99

T
PLEASU
PRINCIPL

A novel by
Felice Gordon

THE PLEASURE PRINCIPLE

DELACORTE PRESS / NEW YORK, N.Y.

pleas'ure prin'ciple, *Psychoanal.* an automatic mental drive or instinct seeking to avoid pain and to obtain pleasure.

THE RANDOM HOUSE DICTIONARY
OF THE ENGLISH LANGUAGE

THE
PLEASURE
PRINCIPLE

CHAPTER 1

Ignoring requests to turn back, the photographers followed them
from the VIP lounge onto the tarmac.

"One more, Toni," shouted a man imprisoned in the straps of
a 16 mm. camera and sound equipment.

"Could you take off the glasses, please."

She walked ahead, oblivious to the calls, the glasses a permanent feature of the architecture of her face. Some said unkindly
of the martyred wife that beneath the glasses were empty
sockets and underneath the flowing brown wig was the shaved
head of a nun.

"Can we have a statement from someone?" the AP man per-
sisted.

Gavin Southwell, the family's unofficial spokesman and constant attendant, drawled in his most Southern tone:

"We headin' for Mallacca for the gala, gentlemen," then strode on his stumpy legs to catch up with the long-legged group. He was forty-seven, four feet nine, and was the group pet. Indeed, he resembled a poodle gone to seed and like a poodle, Gavin still licked whoever's hand happened to be extended.

"Is she going to marry the Duke of Petersford?" *Time*'s man asked imperiously. His readers had a right to know, not to mention his editor.

"You'll have to ask the lady herself," Gavin answered with equal pomposity. He found himself alone, plump and perspiring; the others were already aboard the Boeing 707.

Gavin climbed the steps of the plane and turning to the press, removed the plaid cap that covered the bald top of his head and waved. Cameras clicked. He smiled happily, knowing that his picture, for lack of others, would be picked up by the wire services and he'd have a batch of clippings to paw through on his return. The service had missed one from the *Santa Ana Chronicle* last week, and he had given them hell.

The stewardess, a happy blonde with an enormous bust, gave Gavin a dazzling white smile as she took his coat. He gazed around at the first-class section: except for their party, consisting of Toni, Deborah, Lord Nikolas Kostrjnski, the Duke and himself, it would be empty. He stood for a moment in the aisle, looking at the group; Toni and Deborah were sitting together and it again flashed through Gavin's mind how much the sisters looked alike. The Duke was approaching the champagne in the cooler. Gavin sat down beside Nick.

"Arki thinks of everything . . . such a busy man and yet so thoughtful," Nick said. "He's taken over the whole of first class for us."

"Very nice indeed," Gavin agreed, happy at the thought of another free trip. A week—a whole seven days—was going to be just what he needed.

"Who's got my Valium?" Toni asked sharply.

Gavin took twelve bottles of pills out of his attaché case and offered them to her.

"They're yellow, Gavin!"

"I think John had 'em last."

"John, have you got my pills?"

John Mulholland, eleventh Duke of Petersford, was agreeing with the attractive stewardess that the first bottle of Dom Perignon was somewhat underchilled. He heard Toni's querulous demand, rooted through his pockets, and discovered a bottle in his waistcoat.

"These?"

"Are they yellow?" Toni asked.

"Yes, they are, and they're no damn good for a hangover. I happen to know, because I took five yesterday."

"Valium," said Toni, "is a tranquilizer."

"That explains why I passed out at dinner, Toni," the Duke said self-righteously. He handed the bottle to Toni, who took two without water. "Gavin assured me they were vitamin D, and just the thing for a bad head."

"Poor little you," Gavin said under his breath.

"My hundred," Toni mumbled, "and thirty-sixth crossing and it still scares the shit out of me."

She handed the bottle to her sister, who also took two.

Toni took off her large, black-framed glasses and blinked. Her eyes were light green, and spaced far apart.

"Frank always took his glasses off on takeoffs and landings," Toni announced to the group. "Said that if you crashed and walked away from it you could still end up blind."

Gavin deftly removed his contact lenses to be on the safe side, and Nick picked up a copy of Vogue to see if his photo or Deborah's were in this month. He had been disappointed twice running, but happily the Avedon photos were there in the middle section. If Avedon takes them, he thought, they've got to use them.

"See Vogue, Deborah?"

"Not now, Nick," his wife said, gripping the armrest tightly as Toni did. She was, Gavin had long ago decided, a perfect double for her sister, except for the wigs: if Toni wore a long one, Deborah's would be short, and vice versa.

"Nobody talk," Toni ordered.

The others obeyed her command, without question. She had been, after all, the queen.

Niece of one President and hostess for another—the second bachelor President in American history—she had long worn the mantle of America's royal lady. But after the death of her husband, whom the President had been grooming to succeed him in the White House, her position had lost its power with the new administration. Her parties were still well attended, and her favors were sought, but now that she no longer ruled, she had lost interest in Washington and in the game itself.

In New York, at River House, the new faces, the movie producers, fashion designers and clever writers and painters whom Gavin introduced to her, served for a time to take her mind off the fact that she was widowed, thirty-two and had done just about everything.

But after a year, she had reached the unhappy conclusion that she had met everyone and knew no one. It was time for an affair and she selected a young film-studio head. He behaved like a schoolboy in bed, and reached his climax in about three minutes. He broke down, crying hysterically, and confessed that he had suffered from this problem since puberty. Toni finished herself, petted him like a child, gave him a stiff drink and sent him on his way.

A painter by the name of Erlatz, one of the leaders of the New York School, had succeeded the speedy executive. At fifty-two, Erlatz had the reputation of being an insatiable lover, a gifted painter and an intellectual. Toni enjoyed his company— his conversation ranged from Chinese poetry to urban redevelopment. He had an opinion on every subject under the sun, but after a while it became clear that he was largely interested in meeting people through her. She didn't resent his social-climbing, but his sex-life was a medley of all the perversions she'd ever heard about. When he brought a sixteen-year-old Danish girl with him in an effort to introduce her to the joys of Lesbianism, she protested, got her unlisted number changed and told her secretary that she was always to be out if Erlatz ever appeared again. Then she began to be more aware of Arki.

Arki was always in the background, vigorous, attractive, and the only man she'd met capable of the grand gesture. His reputation as a pirate in business and a reckless philanderer somehow made him even more attractive. She looked over at her sister, intently silent, and she was overcome by curiosity. Deborah would never admit to having been to bed with Arki, and Arki would certainly deny to the death that Deborah had ever been one of his bits. She admired Arki's caution and discretion. He handled Deborah with just the right note of friendly aloofness. How had the two of them been in bed? Deborah wildly passionate and Arki methodically calm—just another scalp? But she brushed the thought away.

Now they were off the ground and the wheels clicked into the undercarriage of the 707. They were heading due east over the bay, everyone perfectly tranquilized, and looking forward to five days aboard the *Archimedes*, with the gala for "Africa's Starving Children," organized by Susan Belmont—now the Countess of Mallacca—as justification for their fun.

"I can only say that I do hope Susan isn't going to subject us to another tour of the palace's art treasures," said Toni, breaking their silence at last.

"Anything's better than having those abominable twins do their party tricks," Deborah said with disgust.

"What about Arki?" asked Nick. "Has he made up with them?"

Toni giggled. "Arki has made peace, but he won't go to the palace."

"Why ever not?" asked Mulholland, dribbling champagne on his moustache.

"Didn't you ever hear his tale of the toilet?"

"None of us is on quite those terms with Arki," said Gavin, happy that he had found a place in the conversation for what he considered a droll mot.

"Well, he went to dinner at the palace one night, got the call to nature after the turtle soup—they serve the mock that gives you instant runs—and when he went to the john and did what he had to, he found that the chain wouldn't work. He finally came out for the sherbet an hour later. No one ever mentioned it, but when Arki and Susan had an evening of name-calling, Arki told her that he could make more money installing pay-as-you-go comfort stations in the palace than he could from all his diamond mines. Whenever he sees them now he rattles dimes in his pocket." The group dissolved in laughter.

"Good old Arki. He never forgets a kindness," said Deborah acidly, and Gavin caught the glare she turned on her sister. But Toni was already dozing.

Deborah wondered whether her sister knew that not very long ago she had been Arki's mistress. Trust Toni to land Archimedes Pendelos while she wound up with Lord Nikolas Kostrinski; but her parents had insisted on the value of aristocracy, even if phony. Nick's title, like everything about him, had been bought— by someone else. It was damn difficult, Deborah reflected, not to be jealous of Toni sometimes, much as she did love her.

"Have we a decent caterer this time or is it good old TWA?" Mulholland suddenly asked the stewardess, his eyes caressing her fantastic bosom.

"Mr. Pendelos arranged with the Four Seasons, personally, to do the catering, sir," she said, stirring the bullshots with airline precision.

And now all settled back with their second round of drinks. "Have we a movie as well?" Gavin asked.

"Yes, sir," the stewardess said. "There's a selection." And she took a paper out of her pocket.

"Too bad it's not one of Nazem's little treasures," Toni observed.

And everyone broke into a roar of laughter that finally brought a blush to the stewardess's cheeks.

By a truly remarkable coincidence the question of movies was in the thoughts of the gentleman they were all discussing. Nazem was also bound for the gala at Mallacca. He, of course, flew in his private plane.

His face and 310-pound figure were famous all over the world. Small, coffee-bean eyes, a sparse but untended beard, pendulous chins and a fifty-five-inch waistline. He dressed now as a Westerner, but the tentlike saris that covered his frame when he was a king were more suitable.

To the world's applause, he was an ex-king, deposed a decade ago. Even fellow members of international royalty had enjoyed his plight, relished his discomfort, hoped that the army junta would get lucky, capture him and put him to the death he so richly deserved. But he was still alive in that mass of sweltering fat that served as his body; his title of world champion pervert was secure. He still traveled with six bodyguards because there were periodic attempts on his life. He also traveled with his collection which had nearly cost him his life during his flight from Trans-Arabia in 1954. It was the world's most celebrated collection of erotica and pornography. And Nazem had devoted a long life to its accretion.

After the three Oriental stewardesses served him a pound of barbecued almonds and Hawaiian macadamias and a liter of iced Stolnicha vodka, Nazem settled back while the movie screen was lowered. A smile of anticipation found room on his enormous face. Out of the thousands of such films he had purchased and purloined, this was his favorite. Its dubious acquisition he recalled with fondness.

In 1951, during a state visit to England to negotiate oil treaties with the Board of Trade, he had requested a tour of the infamous Black Museum where, for official reasons, Scotland Yard maintained its own highly personalized collection of confiscated erotica. On the tour, Nazem had taken several of his harem along and while they diverted the superintendent's attention he slipped the guard one hundred pounds to look the other way, and Nazem seized the film.

Now, in crackling, frame-jumping, poorly lit 8 mm., the fruits of the bribe appeared. A badly furnished hotel room, the kind that lines the streets near King's Cross and St. Pancras stations. A young girl, nine or ten, wearing a school uniform and boater hat, stood near a tarnished, full-length mirror.

Nazem wagged a stubby, ringed finger at Min, one of his stewardesses, who squatted on the aisle floor next to him. A snap of the fingers and the guards vanished to the back of the plane. Nazem placed Min's hand on his enormous thigh.

"Is this all right, Your Highness?" she asked, moving her hand.

"Yes," Nazem replied curtly. "Don't do anything until I tell you. Now watch the screen."

The schoolgirl in the film was joined by a gaunt-faced, dark-haired man who carried a large, battered suitcase. The man opened the closet door and a naked woman of about forty emerged. She had the unshocked expression of the career prostitute. The young girl shrank back, her eyes wide with fear. The woman seized the child and began to undress her.

"I like this part. Watch!" Nazem commanded Min.

The woman placed the girl's boater on her own head, and Nazem clapped his hands gleefully.

"What a dramatic gesture!"

When the child was naked, the man also undressed. In a moment of tenderness, the woman caressed the child's completely undeveloped body as the man stood beside them, his organ quivering. He stooped down to open the suitcase and the camera closed in to reveal its contents. Objects of torture—leather thongs, birch rods, a cat-o'-nine-tails, various-sized rubber phalluses, belts with brass nailheads.

The action now began in earnest. While the woman bound the

whimpering child, the man mounted her, and the child screamed in pain as he forced his way into her. Blood dripped onto the sheet.

"The initiation of a virgin," Nazem said to Min as she moved closer to him and knelt. "Watch, watch," he insisted.

When the man had finished with the girl, the woman began to birch the child across the buttocks with experienced flicks of the wrist.

"An artist," Nazem exclaimed. "What I would have given to have been there in the room with the three of them."

The man and woman assumed position *soixante-neuf* until the man, sufficiently excited, stopped the woman and turned his attention back to the child who was cowering and crying in a corner of the room. The woman strapped a phallus around her waist and penetrated the child from the front while the man entered the child from behind. The camera noted each posture of pain and ecstasy as they gyrated. After the pace had begun to slacken, the woman and man took turns forcing the child's mouth upon them, and in a fitful spasm, as though deranged, the little girl turned from one to the other, her tongue flicking out like a cobra's spraying poison.

The film ended abruptly and Nazem moved Min between his legs to massage him with her tongue.

"That is true drama," Nazem announced. "Some of our film-makers should take note."

"I wonder what happened to the three of them," asked Min, pausing just to get the words out, and then resuming.

"They were found by Scotland Yard. The man received fifteen years hard labor at Dartmoor, and had his throat cut by one of the prisoners. The woman committed suicide. She jumped from the window of a hotel. And the child was placed in a mental institution where she still lives. What so intrigued me about the film was the relationship. The man and woman were brother and sister, and the little girl was the woman's daughter."

Nazem sighed with pleasure as Min's mouth increased its tempo.

"Ah, Mallacca, the balm of its weather and seeing old friends. What more could a king want?"

CHAPTER 2

North of Sardinia and west of San Remo, touching both the Ligurian Sea and the Mediterranean, there appears a speck on the world's maps. Even under a magnifying glass it is practically impossible to read its name, which is considerably longer than the area it denotes. Readers of gossip columns are familiar with it though. At breakfast tables from Brooklyn to Barcelona, people know it as well as their own backyards, for it is the home of the Grand Casino, hostess to a film festival every May, and whenever a charity gala is thrown it is thrown there.

Mallacca is to the millionaires who visit her what Miami is to conventioneers. A fun place. Mistrals, levanters and the occasional sirocco fall flat as they approach Mallacca's harbor. The weather is perfect. The temperature never falls below seventy degrees nor does it go above eighty-five, even in July. Mallaccans crave clouds, and a national lottery is held every year for the Rainy Day, as it is known, for it rains only once a year in Mallacca. If you are among one of the 29,456 inhabitants of the island you may, therefore, find yourself holding a lottery ticket worth something like $52,500.

Mallacca was originally the stronghold of those who supported the Pope during his flight from Rome in 1309. Mallacca's only other appearance in the pages of history occurred in 1685 when the Turks attacked. To this day historians are still trying to understand why anyone would have wasted men and cannon on an island that had nothing but its climate to recommend it.

It was wrested from Turkey by an alliance of France, Spain and Italy in 1713, and then those three almost went to war over it. The English intervened to settle the dispute, and in 1715 arranged the Treaty of Mallacca, guaranteeing the island's independence and declaring it a principality.

Mallacca took as its leader Count Paul Martell, an expatriate French nobleman who had lived on the island for years and had made his fortune in Mallaccan scented soap and perfumes. Since then, the eldest son and direct descendant of Paul Martell I had become Count of Mallacca in a series of peaceful successions. Paul Martell VI, current Count of Mallacca, assumed the title at the age of twelve when his father died in 1935 of a disorder that the advent of penicillin has since removed from the list of fatal diseases.

The present Count of Mallacca combines the status of king and prince, depending on whom he is dealing with, but in fact he has the power of neither. He does not make the laws, but he does enforce the statutes of the treaty under which, by some mischance, there are no tax agreements with the rest of the world. In the early 1960s, after Lichtenstein had been discredited, the Bahamas put under careful scouting, and even Switzerland had become suspect, accountants and tax lawyers suddenly remembered that Mallacca existed. Overnight, the 1,639 acres that comprised the island's landmass became a tax haven for worried millionaires and uneasy rulers of all nationalities.

A recent publication by the Mallaccan chamber of commerce points out several other details of interest to foreigners.

Divorce can be finalized in three days by decree of the Count. This costs $5,000, which can be paid in pounds sterling, dollars, Swiss francs, German marks or French francs.

One can become a citizen of Mallacca after five years' residence, for a price or by royal decree. But no one is permitted to build a house for less than $100,000, and a building permit, obtained from the Count, costs $150,000.

The people speak four languages: French, Italian, Spanish and naturally English. There is no official language.

Mallaccans can travel on any of the passports of the countries who were parties to the 1715 treaty.

Nor is there any official currency. In 1960, the present Count had issued currency, but when the citizens of Mallacca and visiting foreigners started to use it to light their cigarettes and cigars, and masses of it were discovered in all the public toilets, the Count was discouraged and withdrew the worthless paper.

But there are 4,239 banks on the island. And gold is allowed to pass freely into Mallacca, although a special permit issued by the Count is required to remove it.

Prostitution is recognized as a form of commercial endeavor. Those in the business have to have a green ticket or license issued by the permit bureau.

These are Mallacca's salient points, and they are sufficient to endow this charming island with a unique "prosperity."

Someone once said rather unkindly of the present Count of Mallacca that he combines the wisdom of Solomon, the loyalty of Judas Iscariot and the personal habits of Attila the Hun. His marriage to Susan Belmont in 1960, when he was thirty-seven and she twenty-four, brought him immense notoriety in the United States whose citizens until that time had been absolutely unaware of the existence of Mallacca's sixth count. At the time, Susan Belmont was the reigning queen of Hollywood, having appeared in nineteen successful films. She was known as the Ivory Goddess. Her family was not only in the social register, but owned one of New York's great banking houses. The addition of legitimate nobility to the family's list of accomplishments was its crowning glory.

Susan was a woman who had to be taught everything. From childhood the only real pleasure she had known was learning something new, whether a game, a discipline, or a language. Her day was always divided into a series of lessons. Today it was golf (she continued the lessons in spite of a ten handicap), show-jumping, followed by polo, followed by cooking.

A new field of expertise (one that had never occurred to her) had just recently been suggested to her by Paul in the middle of one of their chronic battles. Following the birth of their twin daughters and after nine years of marriage, their lovemaking had become not unlike one of those tedious obligatory dinners with relatives (monthly!) that most people face in their lives. A chore. "Darling, you're getting to be a bore in bed," Paul had said curtly.

Susan was justifiably hurt. But she rallied. She would learn, she decided.

With characteristic enthusiasm—she might have been cramming for a final exam—Susan sought out a discreet master to instruct her in the subject Paul had complained of. She felt her choice to be an intelligent one. Angelica, she knew, was as reliable as a priest hearing confession. She had to be, after all, for she ran with great tact and imagination Mallacca's four-star brothel. In fact, brothel patrons the world over had rated Angelica's as number one. Maria's in Acapulco, Barnarda's in Havana (in pre-Castro days), and the nine-story Institution in Macao were well below Angelica's, according to one aficionado who had compiled his personal Guide Bleu to these enterprises.

To make matters even more convenient for Susan, Angelica

was accepted by all, a frequent dinner guest at the palace or on the *Archimedes*, so there was no danger in being seen having tea with the famous courtesan on the crowded public terrace at the Chartreuse. Heads turned, of course, but they would have turned to gaze at Susan even if she were alone.

The two women drank Yerba Maté, the South American green tea which was said to have great health and restorative properties.

"Would you like a pastry, Angelica?"

"No, my dear. At forty, one has to be careful."

"But you've just come back from Baden."

"The doctors there assured me that sugar in any form poisons the blood. So I've eliminated it from my diet. Painlessly, I might add. Better to give up sugar than—" Angelica laughed, coyly, like a young girl. She admitted to begin forty but with her long black hair, her glinting brown eyes, the small, upturned nose, and lithe figure, she might have been twenty-five. Men found her something to look at.

Susan looked a good five years older, although she was well preserved and retained something of the Ivory Goddess that had captured Hollywood.

Angelica smiled at Susan.

"What's wrong, Susan? You look worried. Is the gala presenting problems?"

"No, Ernesto is organizing it all beautifully." Susan looked down at her tea.

"Is it the children?"

"No . . ." And Susan gave a small smile as she thought of the twins. Indeed, they were the bright spot in her life.

"Are you afraid that Toni and Marta will tear each other's eyes out in public?"

"I hope they do."

"That isn't like you, Susan. It wouldn't do Mallacca any good if there were an incident. People like our hospitality and discretion. And they pay for it, darling!"

Susan was silent. She rubbed her hand over her eyes, trying to decide how she would speak to Angelica.

"Is it money, darling?"

Susan gave a long sigh. "It's always money. Somehow, until recently anyway, Paul has managed to squeeze through. But now my family have had enough. The last time I saw my father he said, 'Susan, this little indulgence of yours has cost twenty million dollars.'" She gave a little laugh. "I have a small trust fund and that's it. Daddy's been extremely generous, but he and Paul despise each other. He calls Paul my hobby or my whim." She paused. "I'm not sure he's so wrong."

"But Paul has been responsible for Mallacca's prosperity," Angelica insisted.

"Paul spends money faster than it comes in. Mallacca's assets for its size are all out of proportion, but . . ." Her voice trailed off.

"Still, it isn't money?" Angelica said.

"No, it's not." She looked down at her hands on the table before her.

"Then what?"

"It's . . . it's Paul and me. I've failed him somehow. I bore him . . . and he's right to be bored! It's gotten so . . . so automatic. Paul is the only man I've ever known. There was a lot of gossip in Hollywood, but none of it was true."

"I never doubted it."

"I was a good girl. Stupid, spoiled little Susan was a virgin."

"That isn't always a disadvantage in marriage."

"It wasn't at the beginning. I did everything like a child, with that amazement you experience when you first learn that you can read. Anyhow, it pleased Paul."

Angelica leaned forward thoughtfully, her expression concerned and almost maternal.

"We're friends, Angelica, aren't we?" Susan asked.

"Of course, *ma petite*. And I think I can help you."

*   *   *

Help came that afternoon in the persons of Antonio Salvador and Joan Murdoch. Angelica, on one of her periodic talent searches, had discoverd Antonio plying his trade incompetently in Capri and Joan working as a £10 girl in Shepherd's Market in London. Angelica had changed the level of competence of both her acquisitions within six months. She now sent the two of them on what she called "assignments" for a thousand dollars an evening. They performed superbly and requests for their company were made as much as a month in advance. Tony and Joan repaid Angelica with the loyalty of children.

Angelica led Susan through the empty downstairs salon of the establishment and took her up in the private elevator.

"I don't know what you've arranged, Angelica . . . but I trust you."

"I won't betray your trust."

"But won't I be recognized?"

"We shall arrange that."

The elevator stopped on the third floor, which housed Angelica's private quarters. It consisted of a dining room, a sitting room furnished with genuine Empire pieces and an Aubusson carpet, three bedrooms with their own bathrooms, and a sauna and massage room. On the roof was a rock garden, greenhouse, and a heated swimming pool.

"Is he here now?" Susan asked, looking nervously about.

"I'll ring when we're ready," Angelica told her.

She opened a door to a bedroom and Susan found herself in a mirrored room. A ten-foot bed with a canopy was on a raised platform. The coverlet was a medieval tapestry. Angelica folded it back neatly and Susan saw that the sheets were red silk and the pillow slips black silk. She felt a chill of apprehension, and her cheeks flushed.

"Susan, try to relax." Angelica pointed to another door.

"Is he in there?"

"No, darling." Angelica laughed. "It's the bathroom. Now I

suggest you go in there, remove your clothes and have a whirl-
pool bath first."

"All right. You know best."

"I should hope so."

Susan disrobed and Angelica started the bath. Jet currents ran
from four sides of the deep stone bath. She sprinkled some Eau
de Mallacca in the water. Susan stared at herself in the mirror.
Her body was well shaped, with good hips. There was no un-
gainly flesh around the stomach or buttocks, but there were no
breasts either, only two small swellings, with large nipples,
fuchsia in color. Except for the growth of pubic hair, Susan
looked like a girl on the threshold of puberty.

"You've got a lovely body," Angelica said.

"I'm flat-chested."

"Some men prefer it that way. Believe it or not, it's about fifty-
fifty—the men who like women with big breasts, and those who
are repelled by them. But you've got the body of a girl. And that's
a value, darling."

"I tried the silicon treatment a few years ago. Just once, and I
thought it was too stupid . . . and there was a cancer scare . . ."

"You were right. We must not tamper with what nature provides."

Susan stepped into the bath. She stretched out, letting the jet
streams caress her thighs and back. Eau de Mallacca was her
favorite scent and she sniffed the water eagerly.

"You have a body. Now you must learn how to use it," Angelica
said. She wrapped a large velours towel around Susan when she
came out of the bath.

"Now?" Susan asked.

"You haven't got over that deeply ingrained American habit."

"Which is?"

"You're overanxious. Now the next step"—Angelica pointed to
an exquisite china bidet—"*un bain privé.*"

"You think of everything."

"I've had the experience."

When Susan completed her final assignment, Angelica sprayed her with essence of jasmine and a pink talc that was made from a crushed mixture of vegetables and lemons.

"God, I smell so delicious."

"You do indeed, *ma petite*," Angelica said.

She placed a raven wig over Susan's red hair and handed her a small satin mask. "There, you look perfect." She opened the bathroom door.

Susan stopped dead in her tracks when she saw a man and a woman fully dressed, sitting on the edge of the bed.

"What's she doing here?" Susan asked Angelica.

"Don't be nervous. Are you ready, *mes enfants?*" asked Angelica.

"Ready," replied Joan. She looked at Susan. "The mask might get in the way. You're safe as houses."

"If you don't mind, I prefer to wear it."

Angelica took Susan to a high-backed, green-velvet wing chair. "I'm going to leave you, so that you don't feel strange or inhibited."

"Must you?"

"Tony and Joan, this is a special lesson for my dearest friend, so be at your best."

"An hour?" Tony asked.

"I don't think she'll be able to take more the first time," Angelica said, as she closed the door on the three.

Joan pulled up her tight angora sweater and Susan gasped.

"Like my bristols?" Joan asked.

Susan was too nervous and embarrassed to reply.

"My father added a little beer to the batter," Joan went on. She unzipped the side of her skirt and revealed a pair of white bikini panties.

Tony removed his open, white Egyptian cotton shirt and undid the tightly fitting bell-bottom trousers. He looked at Susan and she averted her eyes.

"I feel terrific. We had two days off before the gala. Angelica insisted that we needed it. Got to be fresh, eh?"

"Why don't you move your chair closer?" Joan asked Susan.

"There's enough room on the bed if you want to sit," Tony suggested.

Joan asked Susan to unsnap her bra. As the bra fell to the floor, Susan felt an electrifying impulse to touch Joan's breasts. Joan turned to her, the perfect geometric breasts standing straight.

"Do you want to touch them, darlin'?"

"No, no . . . I don't."

"Don't be ashamed," Tony said with sympathy. "They're beautiful and meant for kissing and touching."

Tony bent forward and let his tongue slip from one of Joan's breasts to the other. Then he slid his hand down the front of Joan's panties.

"That feels so friendly," Joan said.

Susan, Countess of Mallacca, forgot for a moment who she was.

Tony opened the drawer of the bedside table and took out a container with a dusky powder in it.

"Now," he told Susan, "rub some on me."

"Why?"

"It keeps it firm," Joan explained, stepping out of her panties. "Put some on the tip of your tongue, then flatten your tongue out."

"What will it do to me?" Susan asked.

"You'll feel a sensation that will make it pleasant when you want to kiss Tony. Watch me."

Joan opened her mouth wide and then moved her head rhythmically up and down and Susan, unable to restrain herself, sat on the edge of the bed.

She tasted the powder and it was like the pepsin in her toothpaste, only different. Her tongue felt numb.

"Is this a drug?" she asked.

"We're not going to punish you, you know," Joan said.

Tony eased Susan's head toward him.

"Gently now," Joan instructed. "Careful of your teeth. Use your mouth muscles and get down as far as you can and curl your tongue as you come up."

Susan forced her head down, and the sensation was one of such unbelievable ecstasy that she could not suppress the sighs of delight.

"I was always afraid of choking," Susan said. "Oooooooh," she groaned with shocked pleasure as she felt Joan's head between her legs.

In the adjoining room Paul Martell sat up in bed watching the scene through the two-way mirror.

"Has any woman loved you the way I do?" Angelica asked him, as she moved closer to him. "I'm even taking the trouble to teach your wife how to make love, so that you can enjoy yourself when we're not together."

"I'm grateful," said Paul curtly, "but, my dear Angelica, a little more or a little less love isn't the answer to my problem. The fact is that we're broke."

"Won't Arki help you?"

"He's the last person I can go to. We're partners in the Casino and he'll think that I've been stealing."

"Have you?"

"Of course I have. But ask yourself this: How can I steal from myself?"

"You leased the Casino to him . . ."

"For a million dollars a year. He's made twelve million so far."

"Foreclose."

"How can I? He pays his annual rent."

"There must be some legal means in your agreement that entitles you to dispossess him."

Paul rubbed his moustache as he did whenever he was thinking.

"Angelica, you are not just the world's greatest woman in bed, you're also a genius."

"I'm glad you've come to appreciate the fact that I have a mind."

"Darling, I love you."

They both looked through the mirror for a moment.

"The squatting position seems to agree with Susan," Paul said.

CHAPTER 3

The foremost gold-bullion buyer during the pound crisis, the dollar weakness, and the devaluation of the French franc was unknown to the various treasury officials of the countries affected by the run on gold. Various financial publications blamed the imbalance between imports and exports. In the City of London, they blamed the Labour Government, which in turn blamed the Bank of England whose constant outcry was always "those gnomes of Zurich." In Zurich, the gnomes blamed the oil-rich Arabs who were once more changing currency into gold in a panic. And the Arabs blamed Israel as they did for every crisis or incident that upset the world's financial and political balance.

No one blamed Archimedes Pendelos because no one thought of him; not in that respect.

On the yacht *Archimedes*, nine specialists were melting down the sixty million dollars worth of gold bullion that had arrived on the boat the previous night. It had left Lebanon from the Beirut Airport on an Angolian Airways Boeing 727 owned and operated by one of Archimedes Pendelos's many companies. A sixty-foot speedboat that could do thirty knots brought it to the yacht.

Passion takes many forms. With some people it is sex, others prefer drugs or material objects. Archimedes Pendelos too had had his passions. In his time these had moved in a circle: from gold to diamonds to oil. Now he wanted what was outside the circle. To possess Antonia Millhouse was so outrageous an idea that it tantalized him. He resolved to make it a reality.

He was nevertheless a cautious man. He had lost an arm in 1952 in the battle of Crek and he never forgave the Greeks for maiming him. As a loyal Turk he supported Kemal's dictatorship. His support was repaid by economic concessions that included trading monopolies in rice and tin. A superstitious person, he always carried in a pocket of his jacket some grains of rice and a tin key ring.

Modern surgical methods had provided him with a mechanical arm. It could perform many of the tasks of a real arm: the hand held knives skillfully at the dinner table; the fingers could be articulated. The plastic material used by the surgeon had the olive-drab color of his other hand. Alas, the hand could not feel. But Arki soon came to believe that what he did feel with his real hand, he felt with an enormous, even a special sensitivity.

He was, in fact, reflecting on just this on the day that the welders and goldsmiths were at work in the sixty-foot living room that adjoined his sleeping quarters. He watched them carefully as they molded the gold into the ceiling and woodwork. When the metal hardened it was painted a dark coffee-brown to match the rest of the room.

Newspapers and magazines had reported that the *Archimedes* was worth five million dollars, but they were wrong. It was more like a hundred million and was in a sense a floating gold mine, and the perfect instrument for smuggling.

The *Archimedes* was 400 feet long, 2,200 tons, carried the flag of Turkey, and was registered in Libya. It had crossed the Atlantic and Pacific many times and was capable of twenty-five knots. On its deck were an amphibian Paiggo aircraft and a landing craft. Its crew consisted of eighty seamen and ten officers. A hundred telephones connected it to the seven continents. It had sonar and radar and a board-room complete with an international ticker tape which was run by the communications center, so that Arki could get the price of gold in Johannesburg, the latest Wall Street and London stock prices, the bid and asked prices of the world's money markets in Zurich, and any other information that pertained to his business empire.

This modern Croesus stood six foot three, and his usual manner of dress was white ducks, a blue and white boatneck polo shirt, white loafers without socks, and no underwear. The sun had blackened him, and with his drooping moustache he looked the picture of the Turkish cavalry officer which he had been when he lost his left arm.

There were twelve guest bedrooms on the *Archimedes,* but the only one that concerned him was the one that Toni would occupy, and now he took time to inspect it. An arch of white, yellow and red roses covered the doorway. On both bedside tables stood bouquets of wild-growing Mallaccan flowers. On the dressing table was an array of the best and most expensive French perfumes. The bathroom had an ample supply of talcs, bath salts, suntan lotions. On the dresser facing the bed was a Renoir picnic scene that Toni had admired in Paris, and on a silver tray in a small red-velvet box was the famous Blackstar Diamond that had been discovered in the Bar-Veldt mine and was said by experts to be the world's most perfect. It weighed sixty carats and was valued at two million dollars.

No less a couturier than Jacques de Charlus was bringing the gala dress Arki ordered for Toni. Jacques was also bringing

Marta Torres. Arki's face clouded when he thought of Marta. It had been good for almost five years. But then had come Marta's suspicions (justified, for one woman was never enough), her scenes in public, her insistence on marriage, and her insatiable appetite for money and gifts. Arki had always been generous with his women, but he didn't like to be prodded. What would Marta do when he told her that they were finished?

Possibly give an exclusive story to a scandal magazine for which she'd be well paid. There was a Turkish proverb, however, that comforted him: He who throws mud gets himself dirty also. Was Marta prepared to destroy herself in the process or would she listen to reason, to money? Serial rights on a story about him might be worth a few hundred thousand dollars. Wouldn't a million dollars worth of stock in Bar-Veldt be more acceptable? A loss of pride always has a price, he thought contentedly. Simple and straightforward. The problem was that Marta was neither. She was devious and vindictive.

Once in Rome he had two days without her. . . .

It was a girl whose name he couldn't even remember. Someone from the Via Veneto who had been found for him and sent to his suite at the Excelsior. Harmless. After all, he was a man who required servicing from time to time. Wasn't that normal?

The girl hadn't been a professional. She was hungry and enthusiastic, virtues possessed only by the amateur, and Arki took a particular delight in ordering her dinner, filling her handbag with packs of thousand-lire notes so that she broke the lock when she tried to close it. They had played an amusing game after dinner.

Arki crumpled up ten thousand-lire notes and dropped them on the floor. Any that she could pick up without using her mouth, hands or feet she could keep. As the girl undressed, she stared at the thousands on the floor and wondered how she could get them.

Arki caressed her and said:

"I didn't say you couldn't use your thighs, did I?"

"But how?" the girl asked.

"Get down on the floor. Squat over a bill and put Venus to work."

The girl smiled and after a few unsuccessful attempts she managed to pick one up. It was all very amusing until Marta appeared, unannounced, and barged into the suite. She pounced on the girl and began beating her with a spike-heeled shoe. She threw the girl out in the corridor naked, and flung her clothes and handbag out the window.

Arki had tried to calm Marta down, but Marta in a temper was like a dog with rabies. He had covered himself with a bedsheet.

"The Greeks should have got that instead of your arm," she screamed. She broke a bottle of champagne and grabbed the jagged neck of the bottle. "I'm going to do the job for them."

He inched away into a corner.

"It was nothing. Just a game," he said. "I didn't do a thing."

"I caught you in time."

Then suddenly she dropped to her knees and began to cry hysterically, and he was overcome with sadness and guilt. He approached her, saw that the bottle neck was no longer in her hands, and he lifted her to her feet.

"I can't bear to see you suffer," Arki said.

"Then don't make me, Arki darling. I love you. With everything."

He sighed as he looked at the preparations he had made for Toni. Was this *really* different, he asked himself.

What had begun as a harmless flirtation with Antonia Millhouse when she and her late husband had spent two weeks on the boat with him had now, years later, developed into a need for possession. He had found himself flying thousands of miles just to be with her.

Yet even at this late stage he occasionally wondered if Toni had set a trap. She could have.

On one of his frequent visits to Paris—Marta had flown off to

Stockholm to appear with the Royal Ballet, and he had slipped into the city unobtrusively—Arki had checked into the Georges V under an assumed name. Staying at his apartment would have placed him under the scrutiny of the servants deployed by Marta as a spy network. But the appearance of a Mr. Carl at the hotel should have excited no interest. Therefore, he was alarmed to have a cable delivered to him as soon as he entered his room.

Arki had stared for some minutes at the bellman with the cable in his hand. Finally, Arki had taken the cable and fished out some change. Was there no way to deceive Marta? At four o'clock a young lady was due to arrive—the six-foot blonde that Breitner, his assistant, had found for him at the Follies. "A Belgian jewel," Breitner had called her. Arki opened the cable.

CAN YOU COME TO A PARTY. INTIMATE. CASUAL. RIVER HOUSE. 9 TONIGHT. LOVE
TONI

Was it curiosity or recklessness that made him catch the two o'clock flight from Orly to New York that afternoon? He had tried to reason it out, and had discovered only an untapped deposit of emotion that he had carefully hidden from all of his intimates. At JFK he was met by his American chauffeur and whisked through customs. All he carried was an overnight bag. On an impulse he had cabled Van Cleef's to send someone over to the Plaza with a selection of bracelets and pins.

Time changes did not affect Arki and, after a shave and shower, he put on a pearl-gray cashmere sports jacket, white turtleneck, and dark gray trousers. Van Cleef's salesman waited patiently while Arki selected a snakelike bracelet made of white gold and embedded with diamonds and rubies.

It didn't make sense, but it seemed right that he should buy Toni a bracelet for twenty-six thousand dollars. As he was sitting in the back of the Rolls, the box securely nestled in his jacket pocket, everything fell into place with startling simplicity. He

wanted Antonia Millhouse for his collection. Did the word
"love" in her cable mean anything more than "yours," or "sin-
cerely"? Did she use it with everyone? Was it simply debased
currency, or something very special? He was determined to find
out, even if it meant a breach with Marta.

The idea of having a quiet and short-lived affair with Toni was
immediately rejected. That would be as worthless as owning a
stolen Rembrandt. If he had a Toni Millhouse, she would have
to be shown to the world in the best possible light, perfectly
framed. That was the true value of an original. Let the world see
it, admire it, covet it, and surely if it belonged to him, the legend-
ary Archimedes Pendelos, the man who could have whatever he
wanted, the value of the original would be enhanced.

At River House, a maid took his coat and led him into a wood-
paneled study. He heard voices coming from the living room: the
billy-goat laugh of John Mulholland, Deborah's huskiness, and
Tony Bennett's melodious rendition of "Corcavado."

"Mrs. Millhouse will be with you in a moment," the maid said.
Arki sat down.

Arki's arrival had been reported to Toni, who was in her room
giving last-minute touches to her hair.

Now, for a moment she sat looking at herself in her dressing-
table mirror. And all at once she remembered the day she and
Frank had had their Bachrach photos taken. It was just after
their wedding. She felt herself smiling. How happy she had been
with Frank. Life with him had been exciting, glamorous. All the
good things. The famous people. The parties. Herself in the newspapers and magazines. It had been life at the very top.

Of course, she hadn't seen so much of him when he became
Secretary of State, but her days and nights had been full. She
had been acclaimed queen. And the real crown was to be hers.
There was no doubt in anyone's mind that Frank would be the
next President of the United States and she the First Lady.

But it was not to be. The tragedy of his death was unique.
When her sorrow had abated somewhat, she had begun to enjoy

the role of America's First Widow. She was even more in the public eye than before. But with the next election, a new administration at the helm, her role changed, her position slipped. She was not quite so much in demand, not quite so much in the center of things. Sentiment can only go so far, after all. There was no legitimate reason for her to be in the middle of the stage. Toni had felt herself slipping and with this had come a fear. Was she to become a has-been, one of those people written up in the Sunday papers twenty years after to titillate the nostalgia of a bored public? Whatever became of so-and-so?

She was young. She could have any man she wanted. But who? The gossips paired her with any number of celebrities. But for her—for the widow of Frank Millhouse—they were merely ordinary. Anyone she married now would be less than Frank had been, so that she would live out her life in the shadow of her marriage to Frank Millhouse. No, this was not for her. After all, she was a celebrity in her own right. Clearly, she must find someone who was bigger, richer, more fabulous than anyone else. No mere movie star for her, no playwright, count or earl, no ordinary millionaire.

Toni felt acutely—she knew—that she was at a turning point in her life. She must keep herself in the public eye. Mere happiness was for others. What she wanted were the heights of joy, pleasure, the euphoric sense of being wanted—not by one man or one family, but by the whole world.

She had begun to take notice of Archimedes Pendelos. His initial impact had impressed her. He was strong. Like Frank. He was nobody's fool. Obviously he was a man of taste, discretion, a virile man who could and would lead a woman.

She found herself comparing Arki to Frank. They were much alike. Arki was richer, older. But in both there was that ruthlessness coupled with boyish charm. Life with Frank had been good. They were the charmed couple; America's lovers. Yes—models of the American dream. Wasn't that it? She—Toni Millhouse—had a responsibility to fulfill. To live out for the American public the great American dream. The thought of marrying a fabulously rich, buccaneering foreigner who controlled banks, even governments all over the world, became enormously appealing.

And yet—was it really the right step? People were tricky. In her role as America's number one woman wasn't it risky to marry a dark, much older, amoral, Middle-Easterner? Should she not pick a healthy Californian quarterback? The thought struck her as extremely funny. Or—an English duke? Or even a Frenchman?

It was as far as her objections went, because as she saw more of Arki she felt herself physically drawn to him. After all, she reasoned, one cannot discount love, or whatever you want to call it. Laughing, she gave an extra touch to her hair, looked at her watch to see that she had kept Arki waiting sufficiently long, and then started downstairs.

When she walked into the study Arki jumped to his feet. She was absolutely ravishing! For him, there was no question. For her, as she saw his tanned, lean face, his hard shoulders, the question was becoming an answer.

She wore a very simple, black velvet pantsuit with a small diamond brooch at the collar. When she took his hand and kissed him on both cheeks he could smell the heady scent of her perfume. As he returned her kisses, the touch of her breasts against his chest sent an adolescent chill down his back.

"How is Mr. Carl?" she asked.

"Mr. Carl is well and happy to be here with you. You're a very clever girl."

"Am I? Shall I tell you how I knew where you'd be? No, I don't think I will," she quickly added. "Some mysteries are worth preserving."

"I like being singled out for special treatment," he said.

"Well, you are special." And she added, "We both are, aren't we?"

"What made you think I'd come?" he asked. And he was pleased at her indirect answer.

"I just wanted to see you and since I found out through my

own devious means, I thought well, wouldn't it be nice if we could be together for a while. You are getting tired of showgirls, aren't you?"

He couldn't help but laugh, and she took his hand.

"I thought I'd perform a rescue operation. Kindnesses received are kindnesses remembered," she continued. "And after Frank died, you helped . . . more than anyone."

"It's difficult for me to think of myself in that light."

She sat down and motioned him to join her.

"You have a request of some kind?" he asked, wanting to get over a hurdle.

"No." She looked surprised and wide-eyed. "Do you?"

He was damned. What game was she playing?

"I . . . ? My dear Toni, all I want is for us to be friends."

"We are, and it's the best kind of relationship." She got up. "I can't keep you to myself for the evening—much as I'd like to. Let's join the others."

He opened the door for her and she gave him a sweet, guileless smile.

"By the way—that's my request . . . your friendship."

The rest of the evening flashed across the screen of his memory in a series of sharp snapshots.

Dinner was served buffet style. Roast beef with Yorkshire pudding and roast potatoes. Toni made a special point of serving him.

"With the bone, just the way you like it," she said, sitting beside him. "Servants' night off. Sometimes it's fun doing things myself."

"It's a pleasure that rich people are denied."

"I refuse to deny myself anything."

"Well, I certainly wouldn't deny you anything."

"That's why I picked you—for my friend." And she had given him one of her direct looks that were a blend of innocence and boldness. He felt it go all the way through him and wondered how many of the others noticed it.

Toni liked to show old thriller movies for her friends. Arki found the diversion charming and watched her instead of *Sorry, Wrong Number*. Every now and then he felt her touching him and was sure it wasn't accidental. During one sequence, she rested her hand on his thigh and he held his breath to control his mounting excitement. When she looked up at him in the darkened room with a questioning look in her eyes, he knew that she was on the verge of making a commitment.

He was the last guest to leave. She'd arranged it perfectly. At the door, he held her face and kissed her tenderly on the mouth. She didn't pull away or act surprised or skittish.

"Affairs for people like us are passé . . . square," she said.

"That sounds like the terms of an agreement."

"It's rather marvelous having a man who's so quick."

"Then they are terms," he repeated.

He reached in his pocket and took out the long, flat case.

"You came prepared," she said, laughing.

He slipped it on her wrist and snapped the clasp.

"In the name of friendship," he said.

"It's a lovely beginning."

As he was driving back to the Plaza he told himself that Toni's years of grief for her husband were now over. She deserved a rich life, and he wanted to give it to her. He wanted her and was prepared at the age of fifty to give up his proudest possession—bachelorhood.

CHAPTER 4

It was just after six in the evening and the Mediterranean was as calm as a sleeping child. Arki stood on the bridge, waiting anxiously for his guests. He looked at his Patek-Philippe wristwatch (Marta had bought it for him on his fiftieth birthday) and found it had stopped. He undid the clasp, read the inscription: *For My Arki—Forever—Love, Marta,* and threw the watch into the sea.

Of course he and Toni would have to keep the news of their engagement secret or else be inundated by the press, and then the fun of its all being secret would be over. Arki lived in mystery, and he preferred to keep it that way. Maintaining a romantic legend is a full-time job, and the more fantastic the stories and lies about him, the happier he was.

In the distance he could make out two of his guests sitting in the stern of the tender which was bringing them out to the *Archimedes*. He felt pleasure at the sight of Victoria and Tommy. Yes, he decided, it promised to be a most interesting week.

Usually Victoria, Duchess of Hampton, was seeded first on everyone's guest list, but as she well knew, she had dropped to number two because Antonia Millhouse would also be present on the *Archimedes*. No point in quibbling about it either. Arki had made the decision and Victoria accepted it with the combination of grandeur and disdain that befitted someone seventh in line to the throne of England. Still, a gala wouldn't be worth the charity it represented if she didn't make an appearance. Paul Martell would be sure to seat her at the head table and that was what really counted.

None of this would matter to Tommy, for he was, as usual, only along for the ride. Since the *Daily Express*'s hysterical campaign to get him an instant title after Victoria decided to marry a common or garden-variety set designer, Tommy had become Sir Thomas Ambrose-Smith, but his title sat uneasily on his head and he was still Tommy to everyone: from his bitter-drinking East End friends to the drag-dressed little poofs he visited in Pimlico.

Tommy was still surprised at Victoria's attitude. She was always so hurt, so shocked. After all, hadn't his inclinations been obvious from the moment they'd met? Could she have been so desperate to marry that she had refused to accept or believe what she'd heard about him? Small scandal and petty rumors surrounded everyone in the theater. If a man pursued a certain elegance in his life-style, it was immediately taken as evidence of effeminacy.

At the time of her meeting with Tommy, Victoria had reached the age of anxiety—thirty-five—without any prospect of marriage on the horizon. People referred to her as the Dowager Spinster, yet more than anything she wanted a husband and children. The ceremonies of public life—opening hospitals, attendance at charity balls, visits to Commonwealth countries as the Queen's deputy—had become an irksome routine. Along the way there had been several casual, loveless affairs, but except for a junior minister in the Foreign Office, who was already married with two children, there had been no one who really mattered. Thus, Richard Davies of the Foreign Office became her sometime lover over a two-year period, but there were few opportunities to be alone with him. Usually they managed to slip away when they were both invited to a weekend party, and sometimes Richard could meet her in Paris. But his family situation took up most of his free time and Victoria got only the leftovers.

They had parted on friendly terms, and she afterward had no remorse, simply an empty gap in her life that Richard had occasionally filled.

She had gone back to the free-for-all of middle-aged Guards officers for escorts, and from time to time there were hints in the papers about romantic attachments, but they came to nothing.

She had seized Tommy as the likeliest candidate who'd come along in years, and she had pursued him with all the tenacity she could muster. Of course, she had hurried things. Dinner parties in his honor to meet her friends and relatives, holidays in France and Spain discreetly planned by friends acting as chaperons. No one really took them seriously and the announcement of their engagement after a three-month courtship raised disbelieving eyebrows all through the country. Victoria, Duchess of Hampton, marrying a commoner! It was unthinkable. Besides, wasn't she about fifty and in failing health?

The tongues wagged acrimoniously. She ignored her friends' advice, failed to judge Tommy for what he was, and mistook charm for virility and an occasional slap and tickle for a lover's throbbing passion. Victoria, for once in her life, accepted promises as coin of the realm, but she pretended that it was good, hard currency.

Still, life with Tommy was better than the void she had escaped from. In fact, for the first two years they'd been inseparable and she had congratulated herself privately on the intelligence of her decision, for she had proposed to him, or rather put the idea in his head and then before he had an opportunity to recant, she had accepted him.

A slow crack, almost indiscernible, began to appear as they started their third year of marriage. The occasional weekend on his own for a Paris production took on the solid crust of permanent separation.

Gossip reached her. A young French actor in the Comédie Française had become Tommy's protégé and Tommy worked tirelessly in his behalf, using Victoria's name and connections to get the boy in with the right film people in London. She'd put him up for the weekend and then Tommy's behavior had become so outrageous that even she knew the truth. The bills they'd run up: a new E-Jaguar for Alain, a dozen suits from Blades, shirts from Turnbull's, a pied-à-terre in Belgravia leased for a year.

Confronted with thousands of pounds of bills, she had protested. It was her money they were spending so freely. She accused Tommy of betraying her, and he denied it, but it was obvious that he was in love. Threatened with legal proceedings when the two men were found drunk and naked in the car outside a pub in Hampstead, Tommy had cried, pleaded for another chance and sent Alain packing. She'd intervened with the police and got them to drop the charges after a psychiatrist friend stated that Tommy had suffered a breakdown and had cautioned the police that Tommy's sanity hung in the balance. Several crude allusions (no names mentioned) appeared in the gutter press, but the gossip all died down after Sir Alfred Machin, Q.C., an old family friend, threatened legal proceedings.

Now Victoria watched Tommy lean over the edge of the tender.

"You're not going to be sick?" she asked incredulously.

"Just looking at the Med, darling. Can I do that without your permission?"

"I won't be spoken to in that tone, Tommy."

"Yes, Ma'am," he said wickedly, mimicking the form of address that everyone, except intimates, was required to use for her.

"Please, Tommy, do let's enjoy ourselves."

"Righto. Your wish is my command."

She reached over and pushed the blond cowlick off his forehead; he removed her fondling hand.

"If you want to enjoy yourself, let me off the leash. And try to remember that this is supposed to be a holiday and not the opening of the bloody Commonwealth Games."

"All right," she said. She always gave in. "Mulholland's going to be with us."

"Meaning?" he replied curtly.

"I don't want him to lead you astray."

"Hah, that's a laugh. If it's the prowling along the waterfront you're referring to, just remember that wolves don't always hunt in packs."

She held back her tears.

"I wish you'd take that soppy hurt look off your face."

"You put it there, Tommy, and you can take it off."

"Just give a horse his head once in a while and you'll still find yourself in the saddle."

"Is that what you think of me, really?"

"I don't think anything. All I know is that the Med makes me sexy."

"Me, too," she said, returning Arki's wave from the yacht.

"Well, good luck and all the rest," Tommy said and stood up as the tender came alongside the *Archimedes*.

Arki extended his hand to help them aboard and Victoria noted with pleasure the salty outdoor smell of his cheek.

"How are you, Victoria?"

"Right as rain," Tommy answered. "She'll outlive all of us."

"Hello, Tommy." Arki was irritated by Tommy's sarcasm, but his mood changed instantly when the Sparks came up to him.

"They're on the seaplane, Mr. Pendelos. Control Tower just called through."

Arki broke into his broad, white-toothed smile.

"Why don't you and Tommy take a look at your quarters and perhaps have a swim if you like." He indicated the pool just ahead of them. "Do forgive me for not joining you just yet." He raised his field glasses to look at a faraway speck just making its way over the top of Grand Lucullus.

"Remarkable facility, he has," Tommy said to Victoria as they moved out of earshot, "for turning off whenever it suits him."

"Perhaps your conversation has that effect on him."

From the deck the seaplane looked like a clumsy combination of mammal and reptile. As it slowly descended, Arki watched nervously, fearing that something might go wrong. Curiously he never thought of such things when he was flying, but now that Toni had become a part of his life, he wanted her delivered in perfect condition. The plane skirted down, making a good landing. The pilot revved the engines into reverse, then eased close to the boat. Arki waved with the abandon of a parent welcoming a returned child. They were now alongside and seamen busily clustered around the gangway to prepare for the passengers. Orders were barked and ropes expertly secured.

Toni was the first to disembark, and Arki felt an odd, muscular jerk at the back of his neck. He hadn't seen her for weeks. She blew a kiss as she climbed up the gangway.

"I was worried," he said gently. "You were two hours late."

"I thought you had some influence with the airline."

"Not even I can control air traffic," he protested. "You must be exhausted."

"I wouldn't mind a shower and a change of clothes," Toni said.

"Who said you were difficult to please?" He led her down to the master suites. "They're still preparing your cabin, so you can use mine."

She was tired and gave him a wan smile. She looked at his white ducks and battered tennis sneakers.

"They'll have to go," she said of the sneakers.

"They remind me of my humble beginnings," he replied with amusement.

"You've never had humble beginnings."

"I know that, but the world doesn't." He pressed her close to him and kissed her neck.

"I'm hot and sweaty."

"It doesn't worry me. I haven't been brainwashed by American commercials."

"I have."

She liked his tall, lean frame. His hands were rough and he had the appearance of a healthy sailor, accustomed to hard work.

"I'll wait for you on deck," he said casually.

A maid came in to unpack Toni's cases, and Arki, with a little nod, left.

A hot bath followed by a cool shower relieved her of the aching tiredness of the eleven-hour flight. Her clothes were laid out on Arki's enormous canopied bed, and she selected a blue and white sailor suit. The bell-bottoms had been slightly tapered so that they didn't flap so much against her ankles. She made up her face carefully, accentuating the eyeline to make her eyes larger and applying a pale lipstick. She checked herself critically in the mirror and felt a curious wave of excitement as she made her way on deck. Arki's reaction told her that she had succeeded in looking beautiful.

They had a quiet supper of cold, fresh salmon, sliced meats and salad, served with a perfectly chilled Chablis. She drank too much wine in an effort to overcome the headache that had descended on her. A good night's sleep would set her straight. She hoped that Arki wouldn't want to stay up talking late into the night. She declined coffee and yawned several times, which was a signal for Gavin and the others to get up and retire. That was the drill for professional guests.

Gavin had hoped to stay up until the wee hours catching up on London scandal with Tommy Ambrose-Smith, but the Duchess insisted on having an early night. She'd keep a close watch on the two of them. Still, they might slip away for an hour when they were ashore.

Tommy kept a small mews house in Putney which Victoria didn't know about, and he and Gavin had spent several afternoons together there on Gavin's last trip to London. Two young cockney boys, whom Ambrose-Smith kept, completed the quartet. Gavin still had embarrassing but pleasurable dreams about the experience.

Mulholland was dismissed with a nod by Arki, as befitted employer dealing with employee. He had been Toni's escort for three years and had been on Arki's payroll for the past few months—an unofficial spy performing official duties. He was the right name in the columns, and for an age in which privacy was a pure fantasy, John Mulholland was the perfect public companion. He nodded to Arki, and kissed Toni's hand.

"Good night, my pet. Sleep well."

Nick and Deborah took their cue from him, yawned loudly and followed the stewards to their cabins.

Toni and Arki sat for a few moments in silence, then Arki took her arm and they walked the length of the deck, gazing at the startlingly bright, star-filled night.

"Are you too tired to talk?"

"Sort of . . ."

"Perhaps in the morning," he said. "I'll see you to your cabin."

They took the private elevator which served Arki's quarters.

"You're in my wing," he said.

"Does that mean I should lock my door?" He didn't answer, and she turned and with closed eyes held up her face to be kissed. He kissed the lobe of her ear gently. Then, sighing, he went to his own cabin.

It sounded at first like someone in pain, but it was Toni's high-pitched squeal of delight and laughter. He had his shirt and shoes off and was about to drop his trousers when she burst in.

"Arki, I don't know what to say. I'm . . ."

She had discovered the ring and the Renoir painting at the same time and she felt lightheaded from shock.

"*This* is the Blackstar," she said in a low, reverent voice. She stared at the diamond which shone with a larger-than-life brilliance. "There can't be two like it. I've seen pictures of it."

"It is the Blackstar," Arki said with a smile. "Is your door still locked?"

"I can't believe that it's for me," she replied without taking in what he said. "God, the size of it! It's incredible."

"Just to show you that my intentions are honorable."

"I hope you don't believe in long engagements." She danced, spinning like a child around the Christmas tree. "Will you put it on my finger?"

He placed it above the marriage band on her left hand and kissed the long, thin fingers. She wrapped her free hand around the back of his neck, and then she felt herself being lifted into the air and carried. Her head was on the pillow and she held up the ring close to her eyes, and the world seemed transformed into an enormous prism of crisscrossing light beams. It was like finding herself in space.

Arki poured two glasses of champagne and handed her one. She eased herself up on an elbow.

"To my princess," he said, clinking glasses.

"One of the things I love about you is that you're really romantic without being gushy and sentimental." She rolled over on her side to examine the ring in private and he rubbed the back of her neck.

"I like that. How'd you know?"

"I'm one of the world's great neck-rubbers."

"You've rubbed thousands."

"You wouldn't want someone who didn't have experience."

"You've always got the right answers for me."

"Because I'm in love."

She stretched her arms and gave a loud yawn.

"Are you testing my patience? Because if you are, I think you ought to know that you've run out of time." He turned her face to his and kissed her. She opened her mouth and he tasted the wine on her tongue. His chest was against her breasts and he felt them firm up.

He opened the clasp of his trousers and she saw a copper-brown body. He leaned over and she touched his stomach.

"It's a monster, Arki. I love monsters."

She lifted herself up on her elbow and swung her legs down to the floor.

"I'm so . . . wet," she said, then walked rather shakily to his bathroom. He was behind her stealthily, like a long, muscular cat.

"I won't leave you alone for a minute," he said, pulling up the thin blouse she was wearing. When he couldn't get to the buttons, he simply ripped it down the back and yanked it off her.

"I feel as if I'm being raped."

"You are."

She managed to get to the zipper of her trousers before he did and as they dropped on the floor, he grabbed her in a viselike hold. She tried to stop him and begged him to allow her to use the bidet in private for a minute, but he ignored her and stripped off the white panties. She almost fell and he caught her and sat her down on the bidet. He turned the tap and spread her legs. Then, kneeling, he took a scented towel, wet it and began to douche her. She sat there helplessly, staring at the diamond while she had another orgasm. God, wouldn't he stop for a minute and let her catch her breath?

He dried her with the fussiness of an attendant in a health spa.

"I'm not used to—"

"Making love," he replied quickly.

"No. Being attacked like an animal."

"I suppose Frank asked your permission every time."

"We managed very well, believe me," she said angrily.

The expression on his face changed to one of shock and disappointment.

"I wasn't expecting that."

"Oh, Arki, I didn't mean for it to come out like that."

"Who else was there besides Frank?" he demanded.

"Is it important?"

"Obviously it is. Who was he? Or was it them?"

He stood over her like a madman about to spring at his victim.

"Christ, Toni, don't tell me. I'm sorry I asked. I'm jealous of everyone."

He sat down on the edge of the bed. "I got carried away," he said apologetically.

"It's my fault."

She crept up on him and unsnapped her brassiere.

"I didn't mean to upset you," she said.

"We're both not used to answering questions."

He got down on his knees, wrapped her legs around his neck and began to explore the secret mysteries of her body. She shook convulsively, then fell back and groaned in an ecstasy of pain and pleasure as he forced her lips apart and went deep inside her.

It didn't seem possible, but she felt herself about to come again. As she did, she moved him off her.

"Something wrong?" he asked.

"I want to love you up."

"You don't have to do that."

"I just want to."

"In gratitude?"

"No, love, Arki, just love."

CHAPTER 5

The enormous white Corinthian columns in the dining room of the Carlton House gave the guests a sense of privacy. Thus do façades deceive the innocent. Strategically placed at the edge of a column was Carla Fabrizzi. She could see whoever came in, but they could not see her. She sulked at the table as her husband pored over the menu. Giovanni Mosca sat with his back to the entrance, debating over which hors d'oeuvres to order (oysters, always dangerous in France, or escargot and a night of suffering with Gelusil and a quart of Perrier as temporary antidotes). He selected smoked Scotch salmon just flown in from England. Carla wouldn't come near him if his breath smelled of garlic.

Seated with them was Ricardo Ricci, Carla's perennial co-star and full-time lover, who at her insistence had accompanied her to Mallacca for the gala. The three of them traveling together like this always made Ricardo extremely uncomfortable, for he was convinced that Giovanni still did not know about him and Carla. While Giovanni turned his head to order from the maître d', Ricardo seized the opportunity to blow Carla a kiss. She did not react, the perfect actress in public. Instead she extended her cigarette for him to light, and slipped her foot out of her shoe and between his legs.

"Chablis all right with you? You're having trout, Ricardo?"

"I don't know about the wine," Ricardo said uncertainly.

"Come, have a drop, it'll relax you. You look a bit tired to me."

"Well, yes, a glass of Chablis won't do too much damage."

"There's a manly decision for you, eh Carla?" and Giovanni gave them both a wide smile.

Did Giovanni know something about them, Carla wondered vaguely. After all this time, had they done something indiscreet to call his attention to their affair.

"I've brought some scripts along for you to read, Ricardo. One's quite good, the others have possibilities."

"Can't you see that he's exhausted?" Carla objected.

"Don't be silly, work agrees with him. It's a Western—a good one—and Leopold has already said he'd direct."

"If Ricardo *agrees* to it, isn't that so?" Carla insisted.

"Well, perhaps that is the case. In any event I told him you were interested," Giovanni said, winking at Ricardo.

"Is there a part for Carla?" Ricardo asked, munching a celery stalk.

"Not in this one, unfortunately. The women are all murdered or tortured to death when they're not raped. Give all our contract players an opportunity to work, and it should amuse you as well. Several of them . . . well, not to put too fine a point . . . are extraordinary-looking. And they'd give anything to work with you—a real professional who knows all the tricks."

Carla took a deep breath and stared at her salade Niçoise with distaste. "It won't do his career any good, Giovanni. You know that."

"Well, darling, it's half a million dollars worth of art to Ricardo. I'm getting it co-financed with an American major and they've also offered to give Ricardo a piece of the film. He can take the money in Swiss francs. Tax-free into the bargain."

"The script's probably rubbish and Ricardo will have to kill himself doing all those tricks they have to do in Westerns."

"We have stuntmen for that." Giovanni's smile was sweet.

"I'm not quite sure I should," Ricardo said. "I need a rest."

"A week in Mallacca ought to put you straight. Water-skiing. Arki has an excellent instructor. Do some serious drinking. And maybe spend a little time with old friends." Giovanni added archly. He went on. "Half a million. In dollars if you prefer it, but they're not so safe now. Talk about devaluation. He-man role. You kill about forty people in the film, and with Leopold's trick photography and gimmicks it ought to make a fortune."

"Oh, all right, I'll have a look at the script."

"I had the bellman place it on your night table. Just in case you have any trouble sleeping, I thought you might glance through it."

"Are we here for the gala and some fun or for business conferences?" Carla said angrily.

"I don't see the harm in having a chat. . . . Isn't your salade Niçoise any good? Perhaps the tournedos will be better."

It was impossible to beat Giovanni at this game, Ricardo realized. He had signed a ten-year contract with him years before with various options and commitments that were as legal and binding as those contracts entered into by indentured servants in the colonies. Giovanni owned him. Giovanni could loan him to various companies at a price well above the half-million he was now being offered, and Giovanni would keep the differential.

All is fair in love and contracts. If Ricardo refused to work for Giovanni, he could not work for anyone else; no American studio could hire him without a release from Mosca. At the beginning of his career, it had all seemed too wonderful: a ten-year contract with a guarantee of fifty thousand dollars a year.

He had been an unknown theater actor playing minor parts when Giovanni had signed him. He had been earning forty dollars a week and living in a cheap *pensione* with the rest of the permanent repertory players, and he had hated every second of it. There was no fun in being poor and unknown. Ricardo had learned very little about his craft, since the director and other actors were as amateurish as he. The plays were either badly interpreted *commedia dell' arte* pieces or socially conscious tracts by well-intentioned young writers filled with unspeakable dialogue and pretentious social truths.

Giovanni had sent him to the best acting teacher in Rome; he had studied hard and within a year had developed into a remarkably sensitive actor. His voice had been good, and his looks attractive to both men and women. He had a natural bent for light comedy and love stories. That smirk of his was as famous as the Gable smile had been. A succession of films with Carla which had made money and received critical acclaim had established him as Italy's most important actor. But he had found success sad and somehow inhuman until he fell in love with Carla.

Giovanni sipped the Chablis, found it to his liking and nodded to the sommelier.

"The trout is perfect, don't you think, Ricardo? You should have had it meunière," he added, putting a chunk of bread into the butter sauce.

Peasants don't change their habits, Carla reflected. She was a snob, despite the fact that she herself came of peasant stock. She had overcome it by an act of will and her manners were so perfect that they seemed dramatic gestures. She had learned the right things to do, but they still were not part of her style; it was evident that they had been acquired and were not inbred.

"The tournedos are raw," she complained. "Tell the waiter to let me have the trout instead. And for your information, Giovanni, Chablis with filet is a disgusting combination."

"Forgive me," he said, winking at Ricardo. "But when I have a new project in mind, I lose sight of everything."

"Oh, what a lovely surprise," Carla said suddenly, then broke off. Giovanni craned his thick neck around. The air-conditioning had not been as strong as he liked and a wet ring of perspiration circled his collar.

"It's Madeleine and Fritz," he said rising.

Madeleine stopped, threw her arms around Giovanni and then kissed Carla on both cheeks.

"I didn't know you were coming," Carla said.

"Didn't you? Giovanni invited us."

"Carla darling, surely I told you." Giovanni squeezed Madeleine's hand. "To think I might have had you under contract as well," he said, sighing with regret. "That would've given me the two number ones," he told Ricardo, who was yawning.

"And what would I have done?" Madeleine asked. "Italian nudies instead of French ones?"

"Oh, I love that sharp little tongue. I thrive on controversy. Keeps me young, doesn't it, Carla?"

"I thought *I* did."

"What are you, if not controversial?" He laughed at his own wit. "Isn't Fritz going to join us? I'll make him a producer."

"Ask him," said Madeleine, looking over at her husband who had paused to talk to someone at another table.

Giovanni chuckled, "Fine steel Von Kuhl made during the war. In fact I was a tank officer. Drove one of his products. Five bazookas were needed to knock out our Panzer. I've great respect for his company."

"They're making railway cars now."

"As long as the cash register rings, as we say in Italy." And Giovanni rose and walked over to Fritz and his companion.

Ricardo dared not express anything toward Madeleine but fatigue and boredom, an index of his steadfastness and loyalty to Carla. A raised eyebrow, a vacant stare even, would result in a hysterical row. Twice he had been forced to turn down films that would have co-starred Madeleine Maté (the "man-eater" Carla called her behind her back), for Carla's jealousy was both violent and noisy. "The single thing she does better than I in a film is strip off her clothes," Carla had once said. "She holds the Olympic record in that event."

"The trip's exhausted me and we finished shooting only yesterday," Ricardo said, rising from the table. He shook Madeleine's hand and walked quickly out of the dining room, oblivious of the turning heads.

Madeleine snorted. "I think he's probably a fetishist. Goes to bed with a handbag or high-heeled shoes and relieves himself."

Carla was unable to prevent the flush that covered her face like unexpected sunlight.

"He's a fine actor and we enjoy a good working relationship. That's all Giovanni and I are concerned about." And then quickly, "How is it working out with you and Fritz? There've been stories . . ."

"Well, whatever you've heard is true. He's jealous, insatiable and promiscuous. I suppose we get what we deserve. I still change partners when the mood takes me. Our marriage is one of contradictions in personalities, moods and desires, and yet there's a certain common ground. Hard to explain. When I hate him most, I find myself forgiving him and after I do, I despise him."

They sat sipping brandy. Madeleine refused to eat. She put on weight easily and lost it with difficulty now, and since her figure was her fortune she was frightened to tempt fate. They both became giddy with laughter when Fritz and Giovanni approached.

"We've missed something?" Giovanni asked.

"We were about to reminisce on our first film together," Madeleine told Fritz, who nodded to Carla and sat down with the stiffness of a Prussian lieutenant.

"Perhaps I can hear," he said.

"We were both extras," Carla began, "in 1958 and working in a dreadful film called *The Torture of the Sabines* or something of the kind . . . everything dubbed out of sync."

"Neither of us had speaking parts," said Madeleine. "We simply walked about in the transparent negligées that the director thought were Roman."

"We looked ravishing but had to live on Genoa salami, and so any time someone tried to test our charms we simply breathed on them. Virgin days . . ."

"Speak for yourself, Carla. I lost mine at the *lycée*, God be praised in his all-knowing wisdom." Madeleine drank more brandy and laughed.

"Finally, before one particular sequence, the director came up with his single creative idea. To show a woman bare-breasted before the rape in the orgy scene."

"One hundred girls volunteered."

"And the director was at a loss."

"He called 'cut,' then huddled with Signor Mosca here, the talented producer of this marvelous work of art, and Signor Mosca decided that a contest must be held.

"Tape measures were produced. The determining factor was who had the largest bust. Girls dropped their costumes right on the set and the director went around with a tape measure."

Carla could not suppress a smile.

"The director eliminated ninety-eight girls. Two were left. Madeleine and I."

"The producer, his royal highness here, appeared on the set, had another conference with the director and decided to use us both."

Giovanni chuckled at the memory.

"It was a dead heat, Fritz. Both thirty-six C, so I decided that the two must tear each other's clothes off and the one with the least on after the staged fight would go to the American weightlifter who was playing Hannibal or whoever."

"I've seen that photo reproduced in all the dirty American magazines," said Fritz hotly.

"The two of them topless. Such is art," Giovanni replied.

Fritz was not amused by the story and he rubbed his hands through his hair.

"I brought a lawsuit against a German magazine for publishing it."

"He lost," Madeleine said happily.

"The fact remains that while Madeleine is my wife, I cannot tolerate public embarrassment. My family name is involved and it has all been extremely unpleasant."

He left with toy-soldier movements, thrusting his napkin down and pushing his chair into the table.

"You will please excuse me."

"You aren't quite so proper when you're making the rounds of the brothels in Essen, my dear Fritz," Madeleine said angrily.

"If I had a wife instead of a dirty picture, things might be different," he added, and left.

"*Boche!*" Madeleine called after him.

Carla and Giovanni looked awkardly at each other.

"I didn't realize the story would upset him," Giovanni said. "Perhaps you ought to go after him."

"I know where he'll be."

"Where?" Carla asked, puzzled.

"Checking in at Angelica's," Madeleine said contemptuously.

H.R.H. King Nazem, as he was addressed in Mallacca, had the two things that counted, a title and money. The title was tarnished but the currency was crisp, and since he had done considerable business with Angelica in the past and knew she was well acquainted with his tastes, he, like the well-seasoned traveler he was, had wired her his exact time of arrival.

Waiting at the airport in the back seat of his white, bulletproof Mercedes 600 was Angelica herself and two of her latest acquisitions. They came from the Convent School of Sacré Coeur in Lyons and both had run away to Paris. Neither intended to return home or to the nunnery. They had come into contact with one of Angelica's scouts in Paris, and the girls had been allowed to buy new wardrobes and been given first-class air tickets to Mallacca.

Angelica had given them a two-week training program which, although rigorous, had at the same time been fun. She had instilled one cardinal principle into both:

"No matter what the man looks like, your job is to see that he leaves gratified and singing your praises. You must treat your job with all the professional pride any artist takes in his work."

The girls were prepared to go along with her. If they took their profession seriously, Angelica had told them, they could lead happy, productive lives. In Angelica were the seeds of the character-builder.

Sweating profusely from the sudden blast of humid air, Nazem had emerged from his plane in a state of high excitement. He had even gone ahead of his bodyguards to greet Angelica.

"You do me great honor, Your Royal Highness," she said.

"I'm delighted to see you as always, Angelica. I didn't expect you to come out to meet me."

"I left a houseful of guests," she admitted. "But for a king, could one do less?"

"I'm grateful for your thoughtfulness."

He was whisked through customs as usual. None of his luggage was touched by officials, since he still traveled with diplomatic immunity under his Trans-Arabian royal prerogative.

As they approached his car, he stopped and said:

"I've brought you a present and I almost forgot." He signaled one of his bodyguards who trotted over, carrying a black crocodile attaché case.

"Your little treat, treats I should say, are in the back of your car," she told him.

"Mysteries. I must have them to live . . . I won't even allow myself the indulgence of riding with them. I'll wait until the suspense practically forces a seizure."

He led her to the black Bentley used by the bodyguards and in the back seat he opened the attaché case.

"A block of the most exquisite hashish I've ever smoked," he told her proudly. "It was sent to me from South Africa and the purity and effects are beyond description."

"You're very considerate. We've smoked Moroccan all year and the quality has been poor."

She grasped his hand with affection.

"I have, well, how shall I put it, Your Highness? . . . something to suggest . . ."

"Can't you be direct?"

"No, this is a matter of extreme delicacy and must be handled with perfect diplomacy."

"Be general then, if you wish. I shan't press you."

"A certain person requires money—"

"And what do you suggest, Angelica?"

"A liaison if Your Highness is willing . . . perhaps for a five-year period."

"Can you give me a clue to the identity?"

"It would be the prize of any collector."

"Like acquiring a Vermeer?"

"Exactly. No one but the collector and his accómplice must know that it is in his possession. Complete secrecy must surround the arrangement."

Nazem's heart thumped as he rubbed his black beard. Who could Angelica have in mind?

"You know how to torture me as no one else does," he said with pleasure.

"Will you trust me?"

"Of course I will."

"Tonight, for your welcome to Mallacca, the price is two thousand."

"We shan't haggle," he said with confidence. "I've never been deceived or shortchanged by you."

"Thank you, Your Highness."

Angelica left the car and Nazem instructed his chauffeur and bodyguards to proceed slowly to his villa where he would await Angelica's surprises.

Villa Nazema rested atop the Grand Lucullus, Mallacca's highest mountain range. It commanded a magnificent view of the Mediterranean. On a clear day Nazem could see as far as Sardinia to the south and Cannes to the west. He never went to the beach, but from his aerie he enjoyed looking at the fine, pearl-white sand that formed Mallacca's jeweled coastline. The other advantage Villa Nazema offered was privacy. Except for the villa occupied by Marta and Arki a quarter of a mile below him at the foot of Grand Lucullus, there was no place from which people could snoop and spy. In a joint venture with Arki, he had bought all the land for one square mile. It was superbly private. A car engine could be heard two miles away as it wheezed around the tortuous double and triple bends, and unless guests were expected, the bodyguards would rush to the electrified gates, where submachine guns were mounted at the privy hut by the entrance.

Nazem desperately feared assassination and exposé magazines, so that security and constant vigilance were part of his daily routine.

Nazem's car arrived at the villa before the one bearing his guests, and he lumbered out of the back seat, breathless.

"I don't want to see them until I'm ready," he said to Rogers, the English mercenary who was in charge of security and all the other bodyguards.

Nazem rushed past the housekeeper and butler, waiting to greet him, then climbed the flight of stairs that led to the living room on the first floor. From the top of the stairs, he shouted down to them:

"Have you prepared food?"

"Yes, Your Highness," said the butler.

"There'll be three for dinner later tonight. You needn't wait up. Rogers will serve when we're ready," he told the housekeeper.

He hurried into his bedroom, tore his clothes off, then got into the needle shower in his bathroom. He recoiled from the shock of the cold water but remained fixed under the head until his mind cleared and his enormous body tingled with life.

The sound of the other car over the pebbled driveway carried up to his bedroom. He stood by the window waiting for his guests to get out, then at the last minute turned away. He dried himself with an enormous turkish towel, wrapped it around his waist and put on a silk dressing gown, which was so large that somehow it concealed his girth. He checked his electronic equipment, which consisted of a 16 mm. camera and a magnetic tape, then pressed a button and the entire wall beside his desk slid up into the ceiling. Now he faced a glass wall which he could see through from his side, but which on the reverse side was a floor-to-ceiling mirror.

Nazem watched and listened as Rogers led the two girls into the room on the mirror side of the wall. Jeanine was tall and lithe with long, shapely legs. She was blond and had the innocent expression of a schoolgirl. Lili had red hair, was some inches shorter than her friend, with a round face and a full, womanly figure. Both were dressed in dark blue school uniforms with small berets. Rogers pressed a button in their room and two doors opened, revealing an eight-foot circular bath. The girls giggled.

"Do you speak English?" he asked.

"Not very well," said Jeanine.

"Two years in school," Lili added, "but we understand."

Rogers ran the bath and poured bath salts and fragrances into it.

"His Highness will join you after you've bathed. You'll find some things in the closet."

"Mais oui, bien sûr."

Rogers closed the door and the girls began to remove their school uniforms.

At precisely that moment, Nazem started the camera. The girls neatly piled their clothing on the sofa, and then Jeanine went to the bath, tested it with her foot and announced:

"C'est parfait."

Nazem watched the two splashing about in the water like children at the seaside. They both commented on the luxurious furnishings of the establishment. The low black tables, the Persian carpets and the jade statues and Chinese paintings on the walls were exquisite.

As they dried themselves, Lili noticed a certain florid coloring and excitement highlighting Jeanine's face.

"Tu est malade?" she asked.

"Non, pas de tout, mais je sens . . ."

All at once Lili's face turned red and she was moving toward Jeanine with a rapt, hypnotic expression on her face.

Nazem rubbed his hands together, unable to contain his emotions, and began to pant like a man after a long race.

The girls suddenly attacked each other like wild animals. They kissed each other, began biting each other's thighs, legs. Jeanine sucked Lili's breasts with fiendish passion, while Lili seized a hairbrush and shoved it between Jeanine's thighs.

Nazem set up the other camera, pressed the button to start it and left his room. He didn't bother to knock on the girls' bedroom door, for they wouldn't have heard. When he entered the room Jeanine looked up at him for an instant.

"Allons, allons," she said, begging him to come to them. Purposefully he went to the wardrobe, picked out a beautifully varnished birth switch and began gently to massage Lili's backside with it.

He was a man who took trouble, made preparations. The cantharides mixed with the bath salts had once again worked their magic, inflaming the girls to a pitch of hysteria. At that moment he was not a repulsive former king whose appetites had to be endured; he was a man they wanted with desperate urgency. Nazem smiled triumphantly and removed his robe.

"Bleedin' room service. They never understand me," Brian Teal said, banging down the receiver on the waiter who had gotten the order completely confused after a ten-minute explanation. His long-suffering companion was none other than Maureen Polley (known affectionately the world over as "The Pole"). The face which had graced a thousand magazine covers, with its perfectly turned-up nose, luminous brown eyes, clear white skin and black, boyishly cut hair, grimaced as Brian turned his attention to it. Maureen handed the maid Brian's dinner suit and her own dress so they would be ready the following day. Brian's new suit was of black velvet and it had required eight fittings. It had not survived Maureen's hasty packing.

Brian was London's cult figure, a cross between James Dean and a fishmonger's delivery boy. The well-publicized romance between Brian and Maureen, on-again, off-again, was on-again for the gala. Brian needed the publicity.

"That's one hundred and twenty quid's worth of suit that's down the drain, Mo," he said as though of a departed relative.

"I thought you'd get your man to pack for you. You know I was working on that pantyhose ad till we had to leave."

He ignored the explanation and said:

"Fancy a walk along the front?"

"Whatever you like."

"We can stop off and get a bite at one of the caffs."

"Suits me . . . And Brian, I'm sorry about the packing. But there wasn't enough room in your case. I'll pick up a couple of those Italian cowhide ones when I go to Venice."

"That's a good idea."

He stared out at the promenade and sighed when he saw the medley of lights coming from the boats anchored in the harbor.

"I'd like to be on the *Archimedes*. I could give Ambrose-Smith a tinkle and wangle an invitation." He thought again. "No, I can't do that. Victoria'll think I'm after his lily-white arse. Can't have that, not with her royal highness."

"I've been invited to the *Archimedes*," Maureen said brightly, hoping to improve his mood.

"You on your own," he stormed. "All that bloody Turk wants to do is ball you."

"Brian, that's filthy."

"Well, what's he want then? Some of your sparklin' conversation . . . your fantastic wit and wisdom? Give him a blow job and he'll give you stock in one of his companies . . . I can get all the women I like if I wanted to, but no, I stick with you."

"I know you do, Brian," she said. "Of course I wouldn't go without you."

The sea breeze on the Coronet Walk was warm and fresh. How long had they been together, Maureen wondered as they walked. Three years, or four? And all of it had been a nightmare of dissatisfaction personally and sexually for her. Despite the fact that he was just about the most disagreeable man she'd ever known, she could not overcome her attraction to him.

He had had one early film success and thereafter his career had gone steadily downhill. Obsessed with himself, his clothes, looks, facial expressions (he practiced all the Brando and Dean grimaces in the mirror), he had the sense to realize that unless he soon did a worthwhile film he'd be written off as simply another tax loss by the studios.

Maureen suffered in silence.

Often she wanted to protest, or walk out, but she harbored the belief that she herself was worthless. God had given her a pole-like, six-foot body, a pouting mouth, small breasts, all of which somehow in the crazy composition of female assets were welded together and, inexplicably, formed beauty that was beyond dispute. She had no talent, except for remaining rigid for hours in front of a photographer, the called-for expression frozen on her face. She didn't like clothes particularly but was in the forefront of fashions; she disapproved of the products that her enterprising lawyers forced her to endorse, and she had virtually nothing to say for herself. Her one television appearance had been a trial for her and revealed to film companies who were after her that she was just a void of loveliness. But to her public she was still the "Now" girl who had chosen not to talk because talking to people in their forties and fifties was useless. Unwittingly, she had become the perfect symbol of youth's lack of communication with the older generation. She understood nothing of it. Her one ambition was to marry Brian, have eight children, and raise pigs in Norfolk, and once when she had expressed this desire to a magazine interviewer, he had smiled and said:

"Maureen, you're the greatest put-on artist in the world. And you do it with a straight face. For a minute I really believed you." She had smiled in embarrassment, reinforcing the interviewer's belief. It had all made good copy, and the article banner had read: POLE WANTS TO HAVE KIDS AND RAISE PIGS!!!!!

She existed in a world that combined a total lack of understanding with two thousand dollars per hour for services. A studious devotee of astrology (she subscribed to ten such publications), she was a child born and living on the cusp of insane commercialism.

Brian tugged her arm.

"What's goin' on in that empty head?"

"Nothing, Brian."

"For a minute you looked like you was actually thinkin'."

"Oh, give over for a while, will you?"

He led her to a corner table on the pavement of the Café Scotch which was packed with an assortment of young and old, drinking coffee and talking noisily. He ordered two bottles of Carlsberg and cold meats with French bread and mustard. He wolfed down his food like a dog that had been left for the day by a forgetful master. Good restaurants were out when he had to pay. Very often Maureen paid their bills. He would explain that he was "locked into his shares" and had no ready cash. She paid gracefully, bought him gifts at Harrods, shirts at Mr. Fish, but still he grumbled about her cutting corners.

"Got any change?" he asked.

"Brian, I left in such a rush that I've got only ten bob with me."

He slammed his fist down on the table.

"I'm payin' for this caper, then, am I?"

She shrugged fretfully.

"Well, I don't know what to do . . ."

"Brought your checkbook?"

"No, it's at the flat."

"But you've got an account in one of these banks down here, haven't you?" he insisted.

"A few thousand pounds in French money."

"Fine, you present your passport and they'll let you withdraw. They know you at the bank?"

"It's Credit Something. I know where it is."

"Well then, that's settled. Fifty pounds is all you're allowed out of the country now, and I've got that."

"How'd you expect to settle with the hotel, then?" she asked innocently.

"I didn't . . . bloody hell!" he said, in a rage.

They walked back to the Carlton separately. Maureen no longer cried.

She undressed, slipped into bed and tried to read the *News of the World*.

Brian arrived ten minutes after she had turned off the light. He began to fart, which was a nightly pre-bedtime habit of his.

"I wish you'd stop that," she said for the thousandth time.

"Stop what?"

"Oh, never mind."

He switched on the light, took hold of her hand.

"I'll tell you what you're going to do . . . After you've been to the bank, get on the blower and call the *Archimedes* and tell Arki you're in Mallacca . . . with me," he added. "He's certain to ask us to the boat. I looked at it on me way up, lit up like a bloody castle on Guy Fawkes Day!"

Marta had dropped Jacques at the Carlton and had the chauffeur take her directly to the villa. As they passed Villa Nazema, she wondered if she ought to stop and say hello, for the gates were guarded and she knew that Nazem must be there. But the journey had exhausted her.

When she reached home she was too tired to call anyone or even to soak in a tub. The servants were told that no one was expected for dinner.

The crisp sheets felt good against her skin, and she forced herself to relax. She remembered what a doctor friend had advised her to do if she couldn't sleep. "Try to think and see the color black." Straining to exclude everything from her mind, she finally reached the state of perfect darkness.

But gradually a face appeared on the black curtain of her mind and in spite of her efforts to remove it, it became larger and larger, pushing away the black, until none of it remained.

Toni's face.

Marta suppressed a cry. Arki, she knew, responded only to a show of strength. Indifference drove him to foolish excesses, for he could not understand the absence of a response, even though this was the very tactic he himself employed so brilliantly in his business dealings. She gasped with excitement and opened her eyes.

That was the way back. She had found it. Then she sat back against the headboard and bit her lip sorrowfully. At the same moment that she had decided on her plan, she had the consuming suspicion that it was too late.

CHAPTER 6

At precisely five A.M. a figure in a black scuba suit dove off the side of the swaying *Archimedes*. The first mate on the bridge watched but did not react, nor did the six men on security. They had all seen the familiar emblem on the diver's left side. A-P, elided to form a symbol that might have been more at home in physics or calculus. Unmistakably, Arki. The distance to the Villa Marta was about 300 yards and by going this way he avoided the fishing boats starting out for their catch. If he had used the tender, there would be gossip that eventually would filter back to the guests or even the palace. And of course, the newsmen who followed him like a plague of locusts had to be outsmarted.

He was a strong swimmer and the fins and face mask with the air tube helped him make good time. He climbed ashore at the end of the dock and removed his fins, then walked barefoot up the stone steps which led into the villa grounds. It had been built with an eye to secrecy, and during his occupancy two guards on a twenty-four-hour shift would have prevented a casual swimmer from walking in the way he was now.

But Marta had no desire for intrigue or conspiracy. She thrived on exposure, and during their time together, she had exposed him and their relationship to the canons of mass media, thereby damaging the climate of his business affairs. The announcement of a company chairman's visit, whether in the press or through local gossip, always affected the stock position he had taken, so if he were buying, selling, or taking over a concern, secrecy was required. Yet with Marta, there was always a visiting reporter or photographer, or a TV company wanting an interview, and Marta refused to turn them away empty-handed.

What made matters worse was that he now found himself the subject of gossip columns and cartoonists' lampoons. His angular figure and thin nose were perfect fodder to the newspaper artists of the world who had him on horseback with raddled armor, a dissolute Don Quixote figure, or in pirate's garb, brandishing a sword, or sitting in a counting house with the world's riches at his feet. He had been reputed to be a moneylender, Arab financier, friend to Israel, armorer of the Turks in their constant struggle with the Greeks, puppetmaster of the world's oil and money markets. Constant denials by his public relations office only served to confirm what the world suspected. No comment became the best answer to all inquiries. At the same time, he thrived on the legend that he had become.

Libel suits were out, so was invasion of privacy. There were simply too many people to sue and he would find himself in a spider's web of litigation. How could he sue a German magazine for a telephoto shot of him kissing Marta on their private beach without taking action against the British papers, the French, Italian and American presses as well?

He left it alone, hoping that the exposure she had brought

him would succumb to public boredom. The divorce suit that Marta had lost had revived interest in him, and he had found himself refusing invitations to dinner with friends, avoiding his favorite clubs and restaurants, staying in obscure hotels outside the cities he loved. He could survive in New York City only by staying in Connecticut and taking a private helicopter to the top of the Pan-Am Building, and from there hustling to his suite at the Plaza. It became a continual and tiring game of hide-and-seek with new stratagems devised to protect his privacy, which had become more theoretical than actual.

Three unauthorized biographies with him as their subject had appeared. All were the ill-written hackwork of reporters trying to pick up some easy money at his expense. The most damaging had been written by a French journalist and called *The Secret World of the Turk*. The constant repetition of the word "Turk" had made it sound like "Jap." There were also some photographs of bare-breasted starlets waving from the deck of the boat, so that readers would draw the conclusion that he spent his time indulging in orgies. When the photo had been taken, he was not even aboard, and the girls, desperate for publicity, had been the guests of Paul Martell, who had asked to use the boat for a party.

The compensation for all this notoriety had reached the point of diminishing returns.

He simply was finished with Marta and ready for Toni.

Three wild-eyed Dobermans ran toward him with snapping, angry jaws. He petted them fondly and they responded to his voice and touch. He had trained them years before when he lived in the villa, and they would have torn any intruder apart. They followed him to the side door. He looked at the deserted garden in the rear, remembering all the afternoons spent watching Marta practice on the small, wooden platform he had had built for her.

He left his scuba gear in the downstairs bathroom and changed into a pair of white ducks and blue polo shirt. He had forgotten that there were still so many personal things that had to be moved out. Now he went swiftly up to her room.

Standing over her while she slept, he felt a curious wave of apprehension. It was the kind of sensation he experienced when he ran into old friends who were not doing well and wouldn't accept help or a loan. Marta stirred, then rolled over on her side.

"Arki?" She had opened her eyes and was looking at him critically. "I expected you last night."

He sat down on the edge of the bed and held her sleep-warm hand in his.

"Good morning, *ma petite.*"

"Your hair's wet. Have you been in the sea?"

"Yes, I swam from the boat. I don't get a great deal of exercise—"

"And no one spotted you that way," she interjected.

"That was my intention."

"Why weren't you at the airport last night?" she asked, deciding to play dumb.

"I had business meetings on board. And you didn't wire or call."

"Silly me. How did you know that I'd be in then?"

"One of the servants phoned the boat last night and left word that you had come down."

"Oh, Arki, you've always got the right answer."

He shrugged his shoulders innocently.

"I do the right thing and then suffer for my actions."

"Let me up so that I can brush my teeth."

She slid out of bed and he saw through her nightdress without intending to. In the bathroom she brushed her teeth, played with the Water Pik and gargled with Docteur Pierre. He liked the licorice smell it gave off.

"Good heavens," she called out, "it's only five thirty. Why're you up so early? Must have a full day, eh?" She came out, smelling wonderfully fresh, and kissed him on the mouth.

"You look very good, Marta."

"Is that what you came here to tell me at this hour?"

"You're the only one who can put me on the defensive."

It was more difficult than he thought it would be.

"Darling, you're usually so concise when you have an announcement to make," she said calmly. "It's one of the things I admire about you. The way you carefully think things out."

"I don't know what your spies have told you."

"Just the usual rumors about you."

"I prefer to deal with facts."

"What are they, Arki?"

"I've made a decision . . ." She watched him like a mongoose studying a cobra, and he found it disconcerting. Someone had once told him that when you want to end it with a woman, stop off first at Van Cleef's for a bracelet, then go to lunch or dinner at the most fashionable restaurant, where both parties are well known, and then suddenly, over the caviar, fire from the hip. In the past he had used this technique with great success.

"There is to be no marriage," she stated.

He was somewhat confused—no marriage to Toni or to her?

"I'm not quite sure what you mean."

"Us. You and me, *mon vieux*," she said. "We aren't going to be married. Isn't that what you came to tell me?"

"That was one of the things I had in mind."

"No doubt there are logical reasons for your decision."

"We've gone too far to get married."

"And you're prepared to be generous, I presume," she said quickly.

He felt that he had lost control of the situation.

"You've got the villa, your furs and jewelry. Worth around a half-million dollars."

"You sound like a man in a finance company interviewing someone in arrears."

"I didn't mean it to seem—" He paused.

"So cold-blooded?"

"Business arrangements appear that way."

"What else? I interrupted you at the interesting part."

"I've also placed in your name half a million dollars worth of shares in the Bar-Veldt Diamond Corporation. The shares could easily double or treble by the end of the year. I've received word that the surveyors have hit a rich new vein which wasn't even on the survey. So far the quality of the diamonds is higher than any they've found before."

"I'd call that extremely generous," she said, smiling unexpectedly. "You certainly look after your friends."

"You've given me love and loyalty. Can I do less?"

"May the prisoner have one final request?"

"Name it."

"I'd like you to make love to me for the last time."

He felt oddly fearful.

"I still find you extremely desirable," he began.

"Then take your clothes off, Arki. The least I can do is repay your kindness."

He stood in the middle of the room, mired in indecision; then, taking in the musky smell her sleep and body had given the room, he felt a sudden strong desire.

It was good because it was impulsive and he liked it best in the morning on an empty stomach. His mind was uncluttered and his body fresh and he was like a young man again. He and Marta had had five years together and if they all had been as successful as that morning he wouldn't have strayed.

There was something gratifying about familiarity. Marta knew exactly what to do to please him. She moved on top of him, and twisted her hips, trying to coax every bit of energy out of him. She rubbed her breasts against his face, taunting him. It was all over quickly and she lay back in his arms.

As he dressed, she stood naked by the window, looking calmly into the garden. She was smiling, and he found himself irritated by her attitude. He had expected hysteria; instead she had made love skillfully, with just the right note of passion, and now she was relaxed, coolly gazing out at the view of the sea beyond the garden. He couldn't understand the icy change in her manner. Was she pretending? Had she wanted him to end it? He rubbed his chin thoughtfully, then went up behind her, touching her bare shoulders.

"We've been happy together. It was good for a long time," he said.

"Obviously you weren't as happy as you expected to be."

"People change over a period of time."

"Don't try to justify yourself. Not with Marta. You're just adding a new piece to your collection."

He wondered for an instant if there wasn't some truth to her remark. His attraction to Marta had at the beginning been shaped by the fact that she was indisputably the world's prima ballerina, a woman whose art had made her almost unapproachable. Perhaps Marta was right in a sense and he was trading a maharajah's prize ruby for the world's most celebrated diamond. Would he eventually tire of Toni when her behavior became predictable, and she had lost her air of mystery?

She turned to look directly at him now and he noted the high color in her face.

"You simply want a little novelty," she said. "Women buy earrings or costume jewelry, you bought yourself a new toy. You were ready for a change and that would have been impossible if you married me. So, knowing you as I do, my dear, I expect you weighed the pros and cons and picked Toni because she was available and different. She can change your image for a while, introduce you to members of the government in America. You do a lot of business there and they wouldn't give you the right time, but with her you'll be accepted and feted."

"I must say that I hadn't worked things out with that much logic."

"Well, you should have."

He placed his gold house-key in her hand. She handed it back.

"Do please have it as a keepsake. It may have a practical use some other time. I won't change the locks."

"I'll send for my things."

"Whenever you like."

He changed quickly into his scuba suit and the dogs greeted him playfully as he walked into the garden. He looked behind him. She was standing by the window, watching him. She was crying and he quickly turned his head away.

Swimming back he had a sour taste in his mouth. He wondered if she had also made other housekeeping arrangements. But with whom? No one from their set or he would have heard.

By the time he reached the boat his temper had become foul and he was in no mood for people or social chat. His heart sank when he saw all of his guests having breakfast on deck. There were effusive greetings and hails of congratulations from the entire assembly.

"Darling," Toni stood up and kissed him, then smiling, she whispered. "Where the hell have you been?"

"Will you all excuse me? I have some business calls that I must make immediately." He kissed Toni and started to walk away.

"Are you dismissing me?" she asked incredulously.

"No, of course, I'm not." He didn't like the patrician look on her face. She wasn't talking to hired help. "I've got some things . . ."

"The least you could do is have breakfast with us," she said.

They were standing in the anteway leading to his offices and the communications center. Three technicians were in the room and one of them, who'd obviously heard Toni, turned to look. Arki slammed the door. She looked up at him and he thought for the first time that her face reminded him of a mechanical doll's with its mouth cracked. It was against his nature to be conciliatory with women—unless he wanted to get rid of them.

"I'm entitled to an answer, aren't I?" she asked a bit more softly.

"I don't give explanations," he said brusquely.

She had watched Texas millionaries, Senators and Presidents playing poker, and she knew that if she threw in her cards at this point, she could be bluffed at any time. She slipped the diamond ring off her finger and put it in the palm of her hand; Arki stared at it with fascination. She couldn't possibly be so foolish, he thought. Her hand moved closer to him and he picked up the ring, gave her a bittersweet smile and put it back on her finger.

"I went to see Marta. I had to."

She didn't react and he was surprised.

"I knew you did," she said in a commanding voice. "I'm glad you told the truth."

"If I'd lied, what would you have done . . . and how would you have known?" he asked lightly.

She stepped back, taking his measure, then toyed with the ring.

"I would have left."

The simplicity of the statement shocked him.

"The other thing," she continued matter-of-factly, "is that I've seen experts lie. The big lie works only when it's used from a position of authority." She paused, then turned away intentionally to avoid his eyes. "I'm not going to ask if you gave her a last . . . a last *good-bye,* because I don't think I want to know one way or the other."

"I couldn't just send her a letter, could I?" he protested.

"No, I suppose not. But Arki, just remember, I don't intend to be the woman in the middle. The fiancée people whisper about. 'Poor Toni, she doesn't even know that Arki's still banging Marta.' "

"I have no intention of deceiving you," he said.

"You won't get the chance."

He took her in his arms and she reluctantly let him kiss her. "I've met my match."

"Darling, I don't want to be your match. I simply don't want you to make a fool of me."

"Can we make peace?"

"My bed is warm, my arms are open, and every time you press

against me, I think I'm going to die. Yes, we can make peace."

He released her hand and she touched his face affectionately.

"It's such a new experience for me . . . being put in my place," he said.

She pointed to his office.

"Go on in and make us rich."

"Richer," he said.

On deck Gavin was busily writing a press release and he handed two pages of yellow foolscap to Toni who glanced at it without interest.

"Is it right?" Gavin asked.

"I think we'd best wait for Arki to see it."

Gavin's face puckered moodily. He didn't accept editing from anyone, least of all from someone who wouldn't know one end of an English sentence from another. The price of a free holiday didn't include swallowing one's professional pride. Or did it?

There was a stack of reports on Arki's desk. As he entered his office, two assistants were summarizing the reports on small index cards. He nodded his head and sat down.

"I'm holding three calls for you, sir," Pinot said. He was fortyish, thin, and had been with Arki for fifteen years. Arki had discovered him teaching mathematics at the Polytechnique and living on a pittance. "One of the messages, number six, is a real surprise, and I'd like to call your attention to it."

His other assistant, Breitner, was a young Swiss lawyer and accountant who had worked in a bank in Zurich as the *direktor*'s personal aide. Outsiders would have been surprised to learn that with all the talent available, it was these two who so often contributed to the various decisions for Arki's business empire.

Arki scanned card number six, which said: *Increase positions on Central Airways and North Sea Oil, go short on Archimedes Investment Corp.*

Arki smiled at his two assistants and nodded.

"When do we make the public announcement of the offer to exchange shares?" he asked.

"Later this month," ventured Pinot.

"Or next," said Breitner. "The important thing is to cover our tracks."

The scheme was quite simple and astonishingly effective. Arki had done it twice before. It simply involved short-selling stock in Archimedes Investment Corporation and at the same time buying stock in two other companies, then announcing that he was offering to take over Central Airways and North Sea Oil. Proxy fights would ensue, which Arki would lose, as he intended to. Central Airways and North Sea Oil would go up and Archimedes Investment down. Arki would then buy back stock in his own company at the lower price to cover his short sale and unload the other companies at prices that were considerably higher than they were before his purchase.

Of course he was breaking laws but since the order came from a Swiss bank, which would not identify its customer to the brokerage house, no one would know that he was selling his company short. It was also a brilliant tax avoidance scheme, since the money went from Zurich directly back to Zurich. When mutual-fund managers and the public heard that Arki was interested in a company it was good enough for them and they invariably bought, thereby forcing the prices higher. At precisely this point Arki would step out with a huge profit.

"First I'll speak to Frankfort," he said. A switch was pressed and the call came over a loudspeaker and was immediately recorded by an IBM data-processing machine to be stored for future reference.

"Good morning, Herr Pendelos," Schnitzler, the banker, said. "I've good news to report. The mark is stronger this morning. We've refused to weaken it to accommodate the French."

"What is my position?"

"Close to three hundred million marks."

"If we buy francs, what percent do we make in arbitrage?"

"Seven to nine percent," replied Schnitzler. He had a mind like a slide rule.

"Buy fifty million worth of francs, and transfer it to Zurich."

"Done, *mein lieber Herr.*"

Arki switched off the connection.

"We'll pay in francs," he told his assistants. "That way we make a profit on the discount before we start. Next call."

The Zurich stock exchange specialist was now on the line.

"I want you to start buying North Sea Oil and Central Airways. In ten-thousand share blocks."

"How much?" asked Lenzel.

"North Sea closed at thirty in New York yesterday, so let's buy a hundred thousand shares for the next three days. Central closed at nineteen. I want five hundred thousand shares. Proceed exactly as you do with North Sea. Start buying at two o'clock New York time for the next three days. On Friday I want a leak that I'm the big buyer. On Monday afternoon I want you to begin selling."

"It will be done, sir."

The next call was from his bank in Zurich. Herr Direktor Von Steuben.

"Steuben. Do you have the Zurich close of A.I.C.?"

"Yes, fifty-one and a quarter."

"Begin a short sale at the first down-tick."

"How many shares?"

"In all, a million. Two hundred thousand each day. Then we'll close the trap."

Gunderson of Bar-Veldt Diamonds was now on the line and Arki barked out his orders.

"Does the strike look larger than two hundred millions?"

"More like half a billion," Gunderson shouted excitedly.

"Then announce to the Johannesburg buyers and anyone from Amsterdam that the results have been disappointing. Only industrial diamonds. We can then force the price up and sell everything at a higher price."

Arki sipped a glass of orange juice, then had two cups of black coffee.

"There's a disturbing rumor in Mallacca," said Pinot, tugging at his thin moustache.

"There are always disturbing rumors in Mallacca," Arki said.

"This one should be run down," Breitner insisted.

"What does it have to do with?"

"The Casino."

"Is the Count broke again?"

"It's more than that," Breitner continued. "I think he wants the Casino back."

"I've got a ninety-nine-year lease," Arki said.

Both men looked at him silently and he slammed the desk angrily.

"Well, I have, haven't I, Breitner?"

"The Count, however, makes the laws, and he can repeal them."

"Do we have any legal position?"

"Everywhere in the world . ... with the exception of Mallacca."

"He wouldn't dare!" shouted Arki. "I own the bloody country."

"May I proceed with an investigation, sir?" Breitner asked.

"Both of you had better do it."

"You look as pleased as a Cheshire cat," Susan said over the breakfast table.

"I'm looking forward to our gala," Paul said, without looking up from his *Financial Times*.

She felt more at ease and more confident than she had in years. The lesson that Angelica had arranged had done more for her ego than any single experience she'd had since marrying Paul. Afterward Angelica had told her that her financial worries might be over shortly. She'd been so mysterious, and would say nothing more. Susan realized it was pointless to speculate.

Paul ruffled his paper and smiled at his wife.

"The Casino shares are up two francs this week." They were quoted on the Bourse and as Paul had a million shares he took an active interest in their movement. Unfortunately, because of an agreement with Arki, he was unable to sell the shares to anyone except Arki. There had to be a way of getting Arki out of the Casino and still retain his goodwill.

"Susan, I need your advice on a delicate business matter."

Susan wiped the strawberry jam from the corner of her mouth with the edge of her napkin.

"Of course, darling. How can I help?"

"I've found a permanent solution to our financial difficulties. It involves gaining control of the Casino."

"But that isn't possible. You leased it to Arki. It wasn't anything until he took it over. I mean people played *boule* for a few francs and that was it. You ran it at a loss for years, and now it pays for the upkeep of the palace. Without it . . . well, I don't know what we'd do."

"Arki's profits over the last years have been in the area of twelve million dollars. I get a million against ten percent of the net profit."

"So what've you got to complain about?"

"My profit margin should be increased."

"Is that fair?"

"Do you think everything Arki does in business is fair? Dear Susan, do grow up. They say he even raids his company and creates false markets. He's the most unscrupulous businessman in the world. Without question." Paul crumpled up his paper in irritation.

"What are you so angry about?"

"I expected that you'd be behind me. Really, is his goodwill worth anything?"

"It's his bad will that ought to concern you. Don't forget that he made Mallacca what it is. He brought the right people here, and along with that, prosperity. We've a lot to be grateful to him for. Apartment houses, hotels, banks . . . this place was dead until he decided to invest here. I think it would be extremely dangerous to try to hurt him."

"You forget one important fact of life. I make the laws here.

I can change them whenever it suits me. I can freeze assets, suspend foreign rights, declare anyone *persona non grata*."

"The publicity you'd get would destroy Mallacca."

"Would it? Doesn't it depend on how the news is presented . . . or should I say managed?"

"I'm not clear about what you mean."

"How do you think America will react when Arki and Toni announce their plans to marry?"

Susan thought for a moment.

"I still think you'd be well advised to keep away from Arki's business interests," she said.

"What you fail to realize is that Toni is America's fairy queen, and the strength of public opinion can hurt both her and Arki. If she married someone like John Mulholland, she'd be safe. But Arki! A Turk with the world's worst reputation in business—and with women—is just a bit too much for the nice naive Americans to swallow. People accepted Windsor marrying Wally Simpson because that was a dramatic gesture . . . a man gives up a throne for a woman. But the shock wave of publicity, the world's outrage will make Arki the most despised figure since Hitler. The communications media want heroes, certainly, but at the same time really prefer villians."

"And you think this is going to help you?"

"Susan, don't you see . . . if I too am outraged and take over the Casino and suspend Arki's rights here I become someone the Americans will respect and admire. I put my prestige on the line."

"We'll lose everyone who counts in world society if you try this."

"We'll gain the American middle class. There's nothing wrong with their money, is there?"

At the Plage de Sport or "Queens' Paradise," as it was commonly known, Gavin sat under an umbrella sipping an espresso. He didn't remember when he had seen such frieze-like beauty, and the agony of it was almost more than he could bear. That and the incredible heat. His eyes were riveted on the boys (they looked swarthy and possibly Sardinian or Arabic) who were speaking a garble of slangy Italian and gutter French and playing volleyball. Their sweat-slick brown bodies, mixed with scented hair pomade, had created an uncontrollable urge in Gavin. He had retired to the shade, still observing them.

Tommy Ambrose-Smith had been in for a swim and now, dripping wet, he put his cool hands on Gavin's forehead.

"Enjoying the scenery, old cock?"

"Speak for yourself, darling." And Gavin took his eyes from the boys and looked at Tommy.

"Oh, Gavin dear, you are a sensitive flower. I was only teasing."

"Where's John?"

"Gone to barter with the natives. He fancies the blond playing net."

"Oh, thank God. I thought for a minute he was after the boy opposite."

Gavin pointed to a boy with a dark clump of curls twisting down the nape of his neck. "Have you ever seen such grace, Tommy?"

"Only in a swan."

"Yes, a swan. That neck . . . Oh, I get chills just thinking."

"Don't let it pop off now . . . we'll have our jollies shortly," he said. He pulled from the straw and refreshed his mouth with *citron pressé*. "Gavin, love, have you got a bit of the old ready?"

"Cash?" He spat the word out like an insect. "Not much," he began to hedge. Tommy was a terrible borrower, and had to be dunned for repayment of loans. "I've brought my checkbook if that's any good. I could let you have a check."

"Dear, gracious Gavin. No, I don't think these boys have credit facilities. But the Carlton would certainly cash you one. I'll endorse it."

"Is this a charitable donation, Tommy, or just a loan?"

"You're really in a state, aren't you?"

Gavin hung his head in embarrassment. His watery blue eyes began to overflow with tears.

"It's Toni. I don't know what's happened to her, but since we've been here she hardly speaks to me, and Arki, well, I find him less than charming. He stares at me . . . menacingly."

"Gavin, you're imagining all this. I think being constantly around Toni and Deborah is bad for your nerves. You've got to relax."

"I spent nearly four hours on that press release and Arki simply glanced at it and said 'No!' Tommy, I know I can talk to you. You're a friend."

"Speak what's in your heart."

"I haven't spent a day on *Catherine the Great* in the last six months. My phone never stops ringing. Either it's Deborah and Nick arriving from somewhere or Toni booking me up for lunch or calling me to go to the couturier with her. I mean I don't know where I am. This was going to be a holiday for me. And John's been no help at all. He's supposed to squire Toni in the evenings, but he's drunk by four. I'm afraid of having a break-down. I thought that once Toni and Arki had made up their minds I'd be free, but no, she wants me to go to Paris and Rome with her to look at clothes, and I don't know what to say. I'm only two chapters into *Catherine* and that's taken three years."

"She simply needs you. Your advice, your way of looking at the world, your influence, in short, has turned a shallow, pretty face into a real woman. Someone to be reckoned with. I think if you just give it a little longer, she'll begin to rely on Arki."

"He's an incredible boor. I mean to say, you'd think that all that money would have a civilizing influence on him."

"These Turks, you know. Sex and business. Warrior blood."

"Toni promised me a little reward, but she hasn't mentioned it since we've been down. It's cost me a fortune in commissions to be with her. I could have done at least a couple of dozen mag pieces this past year for example. I'm living on capital!"

"That is distressing. Ran into a bit of trouble myself in the old days, pre-Vicki if you know what I mean. Tailor bills, liquor, not to mention my little house, and what have you. Proper rescue operation, dear Vicki performed."

"But you're paying for it, aren't you?"

"Don't we all. Look at John. He's a walking wreck. Brightest man at Whitehall during the war. Afterward they farmed him out to various African embassies. No future, no night life, and strapped into the bargain. Divorce cost him a packet. Scandal would've destroyed him if Arki hadn't stepped in and put him on the old books."

John Mulholland approached them carrying his permanently empty glass, tottering from side to side as though aboard a racing ketch.

"They're going to meet us at their pension," he said, then headed for the bar.

"My face must be a wreck," Gavin said, suddenly excited.

"Declared a disaster area. The old Gents at the Carlton. Sparkling clean. Have a wash there when we cash the check."

Mulholland slumped into a chair, sipped his drink. Seated he could maintain sobriety indefinitely, even talk sensibly.

"Bloody sun's straight out of Nairobi," he said. "Pity Arki didn't put a car at our disposal."

"That wouldn't have been wise, would it, John?"

"S'pose you're right. Still, it's beastly."

"Did you discuss the fiscal arrangements with them?" Gavin asked.

"Hundred dollars apiece and another hundred if we play musical chairs. Becoming a bloody ponce in me old age. Still, natives have to be heard, don't they?"

Both men looked anxiously at Gavin as he made out his check at the concierge's desk in the lobby of the Carlton. Gavin always perspired when he was called on to pay and this was no exception. He had been persuaded to part with a thousand dollars (Tommy had said: "Take along a bit more, just in case . . ."), and now, sopping wet, he headed for the sanctum of the men's room. He shook with anticipation as he rubbed his pallid cheeks with Eau de Mallacca, then spread out the few strands of hair that lived like cactus on his scalp. His hairpieces were aboard the *Archimedes* and were for night wear. Sea air crinkled them and they were expensive. The attendant stepped outside for a moment and Gavin took the opportunity to leave at once, thereby saving the tip.

"Look dolled up, don't we?" said Tommy.

"I don't know what you mean," Gavin replied coyly.

"Smells like a navvie on her way to a dance."

"Ooooh, aren't you both dreadful!" Gavin felt well enough to giggle, but suddenly suppressed it, freezing.

"Don't turn around."

"Enemy planes sighted?" John asked.

Toni, accompanied by Deborah and Victoria, was standing on the sun terrace in front of the hotel. Toni took two steps toward the entrance, then stopped and turned.

"Is there a back way out?" Gavin asked, his hands trembling.

"Just by the side of the bar. Edge back, Gavin," Tommy said with an architect's knowledge of the hotel's escape hatches.

"Are they coming in?" John asked. "Just like Toni to arrive in time to spoil our little party."

"Gavin, just walk backward. I'll guide you."

"Why don't I turn and we'll run for it?"

"Too many people in the lobby. Someone's bound to notice it."

Guided like a submarine operating on sonar, Gavin was directed by his two friends to the bar entrance. Once inside, the three walked briskly past the barman (John had managed to catch the barman's eye and down a whiskey with the speed of light), and reached the side street which led to Rue d'Antilles.

"Close call," said John. "Luckily I did a bit of training in Farnham with a commando group."

As they reached a sun-bleached, yellow, flaking building with the fading sign, PENSION MALLACCAN, Gavin with his usual sense of drama, stopped his companions.

"Is this the kind of danger you felt going through enemy lines?"

"Not quite," said John. "One was never certain of the enemy's disposition."

Victoria had made certain to get an early appointment at the hairdresser, and Toni and Deborah left her at Antoine's in the lobby of the Carlton. She had declined Toni's invitation to go riding later that afternoon. A facial and pedicure were more important than galloping along the beach.

"Did you see the boys?" Deborah asked her sister.

"Uh-huh. I suppose they ducked out the back way. I don't think Victoria saw them."

"She sees what suits her," Deborah replied as they entered the Cartier shop which was next door to Antoine's. "Tommy gets the job done only when he has to. By royal decree."

Toni looked at her sister with surprise. She couldn't understand what had made her turn her venom on the hapless Victoria. Since childhood, Deborah had always used diversionary tactics when something was troubling her. If her mother had scolded her, she would take it out on her father, who in turn (since Deborah was the favorite) would quarrel with his wife. Now as a woman she used sarcastic barbs. Still Toni adored Deborah, having learned early to place loyalty above all other virtues.

"Everything all right with you and Nick?" Toni asked.

"I can't complain. He tries hard, he's pleasant to a fault. Nothing worries him. It's really a gift to have his disposition. He loves the kids and I think prefers their company to mine. He's my eldest son, you might say."

The manager recognized them and approached with two assistants, bowing from the waist.

"It is a pleasure and an honor to see you Madame Millhouse. How can I help you?"

Toni stared distractedly at the showcase filled with an assortment of bracelets, earrings, cufflinks.

"It's for someone special. Have you any suggestions?"

"For the man who has everything," Deborah added.

"Perhaps a star sapphire?" the manager asked.

"Not really. I was thinking of something simpler."

He lifted a black velvet case from a chest of drawers.

"The thin watches are fashionable—Piaget, our own Cartier, and there is, of course, the king of watches." He took a Patek Philippe from another drawer. "The finest one in the world."

"He's probably got a dozen of them," Deborah said.

"But he'll wear the one I give him," Toni said, controlling her her temper. She turned to the manager: "I'd like it engraved in my own handwriting."

She was handed a pen and tracing paper and wrote: "*Arki— Love—Toni.*"

"I'd like it by three this afternoon."

The manager looked at the clock.

"Certainly, madame."

She wrote out a check for six thousand dollars, smiled and said: "Thank you, I appreciate this."

The chauffeur dropped them at the Culotte Riding Academy which was situated just at the end of the Coronet Walk on the beach side. They carried their riding clothes to the dressing room where they were greeted by Madame Culotte, the riding master's wife.

"We've got Araby ready for you, Madame Millhouse, and for your sister, Mont Blanc."

"He's an albino," Toni explained. "I've ridden him twice. You have to show him who's boss at the beginning."

"The way you've done with Arki?"

Again Toni chose to ignore the remark. But as they started out on the beach, walking the horses easily at first, Toni decided to clear the air.

"Don't you like Arki?"

"As long as you do, that's what matters."

"You preferred Frank, didn't you?"

"I trusted Frank and I respected him."

"So did I. But now I'm in love with Arki."

"Oh, come on, Toni . . . I'm your sister. We've always told each other the truth. You've put yourself on the auction block and Arki was the highest bidder."

"That isn't true."

Deborah gave her an all-knowing smile.

"Well, he'll give you everything you want, and I guess if the sex is good—as good as his reputation—it ought to be a perfect marriage."

They started to trot now. At the end of the beach there was a twisting bridle path that led through a section of woodland and they turned their horses.

"What has he done to you?" Toni asked.

"I just don't trust him," Deborah said firmly. "If he could dump Marta so easily, you could be next when the mood takes him."

"No, there's something else, Deborah. Isn't there?"

"Just sisterly concern." Deborah's face was a mask which, because it expressed no emotion, betrayed her.

"Did he ever . . . ?"

"Don't say it," Deborah said shrilly, "and don't even think it. The truth is that he revolts me."

They began to gallop and for a moment in the excitement of speed, movement, the treetops and hedges forming a sort of crazy collage, Toni forgot everything her intelligence and intuition told her.

But on the way back, they walked the horses along the water's edge and Toni looked sadly at her sister.

"I didn't mean to say those things," Deborah said. "I was just annoyed that you didn't trust me enough to tell me that you were planning to marry him. I thought this was just another trip on another boat."

And suddenly it was clear to Toni that Arki and Deborah had at one point been lovers. Yes, this explained Deborah's behavior.

The knowledge didn't disgust her or even make her angry. It was in the past and the past didn't exist. There were too many nightmares there.

"My room is bugged," Ricardo wrote on a slip of paper and handed it to Carla, who had just burst in and with one motion lowered the top of her bikini. She had rushed up from the beach for some Ambre Soleil while Giovanni was playing gin with Von Kuhl under a beach umbrella.

She mouthed the words, "Are you serious?" and he nodded, leading her to an end table with a lamp standing by the window. Underneath the table he showed her a three-inch, perforated metal disk, then, holding his fingers to her lips as she gasped, he shifted his headboard away from the wall and revealed another larger mike with a magnetic back set against the springs. He held up three fingers and her eyes were wide-open and incredulous. She pulled on her top and in terror began looking in closets and under beds. Just above the curved gilded mirror was the third bug.

Ricardo waved her out of the room, then locked the door behind them. The draft in the corridor gave Carla a chill, and she broke out in goose flesh. They stopped in front of the ancient lift which whined from floor to floor on worn cables.

"Can I speak now?"

Ricardo looked down the corridor, saw two chambermaids talking in front of an open door, and an elderly man going into his room.

"Yes. Now do you believe me?"

"I do, but I can't believe it was Giovanni."

"Perhaps he didn't do it himself," Ricardo said, playing with the idea.

"Detectives?" Carla said. And once the word was out they both knew it to be true. He'd probably had them followed and watched for months and now wanted something more than a detective's report.

"I've got to get back to the beach"—she looked at her watch—"I've been gone half an hour." She squeezed Ricardo's hand. "It'll be all right, you'll see."

He let her go down alone, and stood for some minutes wondering what his best move would be.

On the beach, he put on dark glasses. Hands waved at him as he moved away from the cabana area. Heads turned, people whispered as he walked on the burning white sand, tennis shoes under his arm.

"I was afraid you'd sleep the day away," Giovanni said by way of greeting.

Madeleine removed the plastic sun-shield covering her eyes and looked up at him, and Fritz gave him a perfunctory wave.

"I read the script," he began.

"So did I," Carla interjected. "It's so bad that it ought to be rewritten before it's thrown away."

"It's not for you, my dear," Giovanni said, silently counting as he dealt cards to Fritz. "Spades-double," he announced to Fritz. "Here's your chance to get off the blitz." He moved his cards around, joining pairs and a single spread. "Well, what did you think, Ricardo? Isn't it a bit of a lark? Change of pace . . . ?"

"Yes," he said, avoiding Carla's hostile stare. "I'd like to do it, provided the bounty hunter is made more sympathetic."

"No problem. I'll call Rome later and get Giuseppe to hire a few writers." He turned to Madeleine who had rolled over on her stomach and had slowly lifted her head to eye Ricardo from ankle to waist. "What do you say, *petite?*" Giovanni asked. "Are you going to come and work for your old friend Giovanni again?"

"*Pourquoi non?* If Ricardo has accepted, I don't see why I shouldn't. I think it might be fun."

"Have you read the script?" Ricardo asked, trying to fight his way out of the trap.

"They're all the same for me. I just remove my clothes in five scenes, pout, the director provides some mirror shots and we get to kiss each other in the love scenes."

"Your part will be built up," Giovanni said. "We don't make rubbish any longer. This will be a Western in the tradition of *Duel in the Sun.*"

"Never heard of it," Madeleine said. "Was it a silent film?"

"Isn't she precious?" Giovanni laughed, picked up a card and filled a second spread.

Von Kuhl took the smile off his face by calling gin.

Ricardo thought he observed a faint note of amusement in Fritz's expression. He knew it was there after Fritz had expressed his opinion of the project.

"I think a Western would be suitable for you both."

"There, even Fritz, who knows something about the business —and certainly about the public's tastes—even he agrees."

Carla got up, slipped on her bathing cap, and walked toward the sea. She had been had, so had Ricardo, by an expert. Giovanni would see to it that Carla was kept busy with other films; any in fact that didn't include Ricardo. She chided herself for not anticipating her husband.

At six that evening, when they were all supposed to meet for cocktails at the American Bar, Giovanni explained that Madeleine and Ricardo were having a script meeting and that Fritz had gone for a ride to the Spanish Village.

"So, my dear Carla, you have me all to yourself."

"And you have me."

"That's all I want," he said tenderly. He reached out for her hand, and she extended it with a sense of dread.

CHAPTER 7

There was only one car in the world that Ferrari made with a six-liter engine, fan exhausts, a sloping back, upholstery made of buffalo hide and trimmed with suede, capable of doing 220 mph on a straightway. It belonged to Fritz von Kuhl. In Germany he drove a Rolls or a Mercedes like the other Ruhr barons. In Mallacca, whenever he became nervous or moody he got in the silver jet and drove for hours across the mountains, tearing through Grand Lucullus at one fifty and downshifting to seventy-five on the big bends. The motorcar had become his therapy. In the fifties he had raced for Mercedes on the Grand Prix circuit, but the death of his closest friend had made him lose interest in racing. That and the constant demands on his time by the family business. His father at seventy-five was no longer able to cope with the strain.

Von Kuhl Industries A.G. was a monstrous complex which made farm machinery, steel ingots, ships in the Kiel and Hamburg yards, and heavy machinery used for manufacturing tools. All told, something like four thousand different lines were produced by Von Kuhl and subsidiaries. Much of it was exported to ninety different countries. Apart from the day-to-day operation of the company, administered by a board of directors, there were continual meetings in Bonn, London, Brussels, Paris, Torino, and New York, with bankers, government officials and Common Market executives. When Fritz at last succeeded his father he had nearly been buried by the mountain of detail and duties demanded of the managing director.

Fritz had brought a unique gift for organization and an understanding of modern business methods to Von Kuhl A.G. He was also the first Von Kuhl to have a background in finance and economics, and while he barely comprehended the overwhelming technical details which his father and his predecessors had known, he had a modern outlook that resulted in a streamlining of the production line and the various managerial responsibilities. In three years he had increased the company's net profit by fifty percent and he had become the darling of the shareholders and bankers of West Germany.

He revved the engine of the Ferrari when he came down the steep incline of the old town, through narrow, twisting streets which barely supported pedestrians. There was just room for the car. In the road, natives stared as they carried bread, baskets of fruit and vegetables to the houses that leaned dangerously forward like old men with crutches. Some of the houses were four hundred years old and still inhabited. The Ferrari was an anachronism in this part of town. He slowed it to one side, narrowly missing an old woman coming toward him.

He closed the windows and put on the air-conditioner. Earlier, driving fast in the mountains, the air had been cool and fresh. Now in the Old Town, it was pervaded by cooking smells, bad sewage and the sultry pressure that precedes nightfall. Up ahead of him he recognized a familiar gait and figure. A woman walking with a small shopping basket. He pulled over, lowered the window, and cut into her path.

"Can I give you a lift?"

Maureen looked surprised to see him and hesitated for a minute. Her enormous brown eyes seemed confused and distant.

"Well, all right then."

"I was going back to the hotel," he said, "and it's too warm to walk."

The mouth of the harbor was just ahead of them beyond the last sloping house.

"Your friend the actor," Fritz asked, "where is he?"

"I think he's gone out on a boat with some people we ran into."

"Didn't you want to go with him?"

"I wanted to see the Old Town." She paused. Then with child-like enthusiasm she said: "I like your car . . . never seen anything like it."

"This is the only one they make."

"You're German, aren't you?" she asked.

"Yes, does it worry you?"

She shrugged. "I don't much worry about countries, just people. You're Fritz von Kuhl," she said as an afterthought.

"And you're Maureen Polley."

"I suppose I am. Can't escape myself, can I?"

"Do you want to?"

She didn't reply. He found something oddly touching about Maureen. A quality of vulnerability that came over in her photographs. Perhaps that was why she was so successful. It appeared genuine. He liked her naturalness and lack of the hard sophistication that most of the women he knew seemed to think men wanted.

A traffic jam hedged the Ferrari into the narrow harbor road. There were a number of workmen's cafés along the route. Fritz parked in front of one.

"Shall we have an apertif . . . if you've the time?"

He was met with a silent nod after a moment's thought. He guessed that if he hadn't stopped already she might have refused.

"You've parked. . . . No, I don't mind a drink . . . I'm in no hurry. And I like looking at the boats, don't you?"

"Yes, I prefer them to people."

She giggled. "Me too. Animals, cars, boats. Anything's better than people-watching."

"Maybe because you're watched all the time."

"I suppose that must be why."

He ordered Pernod for himself and a Dubonnet for her. The waiter placed some crisps and fried sardines on the table. They were still warm and Fritz offered her one. She was such a refreshing change from Madeleine, who by this time would have been laughing raucously or chatting with the workmen at the bar, not because she was interested in them but only to draw attention to herself. Fritz had become used to public displays and embarrassment.

"Where's your wife?"

"Is it important?"

"Not especially . . . I just wondered . . . none of my business really." She drummed her long, thin fingers on the table like a child whose attention has wandered from the adults' conversation. She sipped her drink and sucked on an ice cube, then when she saw Fritz staring at her she turned her head away.

"Why did you come to Mallacca?"

"We often—Brian and I—have to go to these do's . . . galas, film festivals . . ."

"You don't enjoy them?"

"No, do you?"

"Not particularly. But Madeleine always feels she ought to make an appearance."

She smiled mischievously.

"Maybe Brian and Madeleine ought to go to them together. I could've done any number of things this week. Visited my parents—Brian can't stand them—in Cornwall. They raise dairy cows. My father and I go fishing together. I'm an only child you see, so I'm boy and girl when I'm at home. Silly, but I enjoy it." She hesitated, ate a couple of crisps. "They don't like Brian much either because he never listens to what anyone says. He just cuts in with something about himself. He's only interested if they're discussing him."

She stopped suddenly, blushing with embarrassment. "You've let me ramble on. Very patient, I might add."

He reached for her hand and ran his fingers across her palm, and she smiled, then withdrew it.

"You aren't very happy with Brian and yet you remain with him."

"It's a habit. It's easier than looking around for a new devil . . . Are you and—"

"—Madeleine happy?"

She nodded.

'I thought we might be. No," he corrected himself, "I never thought we'd be happy. I wanted something different. Something no one else owned—like my car—and I believed that I might enjoy it. Everyone I know seems to be falling apart . . . and the money doesn't help. Not one bit."

He ordered another round of drinks, but the waiter was having his dinner and Fritz went to the bar to pick them up himself. He looked through the glass partition at Maureen who was amusing herself by testing his cigarette lighter. He carried out the drinks on a Tuborg tray that was slick from overflowing beer.

"I don't remember ever having more than one drink," she said.

"This won't make you drunk, I assure you."

"I never get high. Brian's tried to get me to smoke grass, but that doesn't affect me. I cough and he gets furious. I'm even a failure at getting myself high. I should be able to do that, shouldn't I?"

"You don't succeed because you probably prefer other things."

"Like what?"

"Driving fast in a car, having picnics in the country, watching football, listening to music."

She was certain that he was going to say sex, and she liked him for not including it, because her sex with Brian had been a source of frustration from the beginning.

"I do like all those things," she said. "How'd you know?"

"I was just telling you what I enjoyed and there was a happy coincidence."

"Doesn't Madeleine—when she's not working—doesn't she enjoy them?"

"Madeleine enjoys one thing—making fools of people—and she has only one way of doing it. Don't you see horns growing out of my head?"

"I don't think I do. They're in your mind."

"Well, probably at this moment she's seducing Ricardo and chalking up another conquest on her endless list. She'll throw it in my face, and I won't react, because it doesn't matter any more. It's no longer important or even interesting. Madeleine Maté is my war debt to France."

It was easy to talk to Maureen. No need here for a wall of defense. The evening before he had paid his money to Angelica, but the sex had been tedious, and had further confirmed his conviction that women will do just about anything for money. As one born to great wealth (wealth that had survived two wars, safely nestled in Zurich, Rio, and the Argentine) he could not overcome his patrician contempt for what some people did in order to survive. Yet he was sympathetic. Maureen was proving this.

"Do you have to be back for dinner?" he asked, with a strange lack of confidence.

"Brian and I haven't anything definite," she replied with a note of apology. "But we're supposed to . . . well . . . be together."

"Does Brian sometimes make plans on his own? What I mean is, arrangements that don't include you?"

"Sometimes," she admitted. "I'm used to it. You see, Brian lives for himself and it's hard to explain, but you know I don't really blame him. He's so worried about his career that if he can do himself some good it's okay with me."

Fritz shrugged, unable to comprehend this degree of loyalty.

It was after nine when they left. On the drive along the Coronet they didn't talk and with a sense of propriety that she found touching he stopped around the corner.

"It might be best if you aren't seen with me. For myself—well, it hardly matters, but I wouldn't like you to have difficulties with Brian." She leaned close to him and kissed him impulsively on the cheek.

"Thank you, Fritz. I'm not used to this kind of thoughtfulness."

"If there should be a change of plan, I'll be in the American Bar."

He went through to the bar from the side entrance, avoiding the main lobby because he was bound to run into people he knew who would ask him and Madeleine for dinner or drinks. Madeleine always attracted sycophants and he was the husband whom they tolerated and who paid the bill. His name, which in Germany was comparable to that of Rockefeller or Dupont, in the rest of the world was synonymous with Hitler's war machine. As the last of his line he had become an object of curiosity to foreigners.

If he could slip into a quiet corner of the bar without being noticed, spend an hour, then have dinner at one of the fish bars that lined the harbor and drop into Angelica's around midnight, he'd be satisfied. The only person he really could have enjoyed being with was busy, he thought regretfully as he found a corner stool at the bar. Maureen was the sort of girl he should have married, someone basically honest and loyal who needed a strong man to guide and protect her. A girl he could fall in love with. He ordered Black and White on the rocks.

Maureen stood at the concierge's desk reading a message Brian had left for her.

"Where the bleedin' hell have you been??????? Waited two hours for you. May not be back tonight, so get yourself picked up or something. I don't really give a damn. B."

She was in a quandary now. A group of men and women in the lobby were openly staring at her, and despite thousands of such occurrences she still felt ill at ease. In great confusion she stopped a pageboy rushing past her.

"Could you see if Mr. Von Kuhl is in the American Bar? And if he is, tell him that Miss Polley will join him." She handed the maroon uniform five shillings and waited by the cigarette kiosk near the bar entrance. The bar, she could see through the glass, was dimly lit and she waited anxiously for the page to return. The page emerged and was almost past her when she called out.

"I'm over here."

"Yes, mademoiselle, he's in the bar."

She opened the door and peered into the blue darkness of the room. She didn't see him at first, for there were dozens of people milling around. She heard a babble of voices. A hand touched her arm and she turned to see Fritz.

"I'm so glad your plans didn't work out."

"I am too," she admitted. "Brian left me a note. Oh, well, it's not important. He's a bit peeved but that's Brian. I'm sure that in his heart he was glad to be left on his own."

"I can't understand him, and in fact I don't want to."

He led her to a corner booth that had high tufted leather benches which gave them some privacy. Fritz removed the RESERVED sign and the maître d' appeared out of nowhere much aggrieved when he saw the table being taken by a tieless man and a girl.

"C'est réservé, monsieur," he said with some heat.

"C'est moi, Jean."

Jean stared through the darkness at the face illumined momentarily by a flickering candle.

"Oooh, Monsieur Von Kuhl, je suis désolé. Mais la table est pour vous."

"*Merci.*" He turned to Maureen and touched her hand. "Would you like another drink?"

"Should I?"

"Yes. Jean, I have a Scotch at the bar, and Mademoiselle will have a *citron pressé avec* Gordon's." Jean bowed low and rushed to get their order. "I didn't think my luck would be so good tonight. Madeleine is obviously busy elsewhere and we can have dinner."

"Where did you learn to speak English?"

"I studied at the London School of Economics for three years. Besides, *die Firma* does tremendous business with America and England."

"Why do you call it die . . . ?"

"The firm. Habit. In Germany when you say *die Firma*, everyone knows you mean Von Kuhl Industries. It's like English reserve in a sense, not to continually mention your own name. The English have good manners in business and with their women."

"Not all of them."

"Yes, quite right."

"Fritz, when we were at the harbor café I got that wonderful feeling I had when I was a child pretending to be ill. I'd stop in bed all day and my mum would spoil me, fuss round me, get me some movie magazines at the newsagent and oh, it'd be glorious. I'd put an onion under my arm to make my head warm, fake a temperature and she'd say, 'Maureen love, if you don't want to go to school there's no need to make your room smell like a greengrocer's.' She knew all along. Crikey, I am being awfully silly."

Fritz leaned across the table and kissed her softly on the neck and she pulled back.

"Why did you stiffen?" he asked.

"I hate public places. People kissing in public always strike me as phony."

"It wasn't me then that made you . . . ?"

"No, silly, not you. I'm taking my life in my hands even having a drink with you. Brian's like a mad thing when I even talk to anyone. I don't know why he should be. Pride of ownership perhaps. Couldn't be anything more. Like owning a block of flats for him."

"Are the two of you through?"

"I don't think we'd ever be through. But I don't love him. I don't love him," she repeated. "He's so insecure that . . . well, you see, he needs a punching bag. It doesn't even hurt."

"Why haven't you been married?"

"Oh, lots of reasons. Mainly Brian's image. Afraid it might damage his career. It's old-fashioned of course. Most actors and actresses get married nowadays, live their own lives. But Brian sort of believes in Hollywood 1930 when male stars remained eligible and had dates for publicity. Besides, I don't think Brian really likes women. Sex isn't his bag. He's so involved with his career and making it that it takes all the sex out of him."

The gin went right to her head and she felt giddy and warm and safe. She couldn't quite believe what was happening to her mind and emotions.

"I feel ridiculous saying this . . ." she began.

"Please don't. You can trust me, really you can."

"Well . . . you make me happy. It's crazy and doesn't make any sense, but there it is."

"Maureen, my marriage doesn't exist except as a legal fact. When I get back to Germany I'm going to institute proceedings against Madeleine, or rather give her the choice. Does that clarify my position? I wouldn't want you to think that you're simply—simply another girl."

They got into the Ferrari and drove up to l'Auberge for dinner. It was high in the mountains and the car snaked around the hairpin bends with astonishing ease. They listened to Dionne Warwick on the tape deck and Maureen thought, I've never been so happy and comfortable with a man. They drove for almost an hour through the perfume section of the island, and Fritz put down the top so they could smell the sweet fragrance of the wild-growing flowers.

"I feel so dizzy and good," she said, leaning her head on his shoulder. "Do we have to have dinner?"

"Aren't you hungry?" She shook her head and he pulled onto a shoulder overlooking the Bay of Mallacca. "There's a small fishing village down there."

"I'd like to go for a swim."

"We can swim just outside the village. There's a beach. And we could get a picnic from one of the bars."

He turned down a crooked little slip road used by local farmers and fishermen to get to and from the town and the mainland. As they drove they could see that this part was shaped like a wedge with the point forming at the mouth of the bay. Small lights blinked in the background. They passed the village square where a group of men were playing *boule* by gaslight. The fishermen were predominantly of Spanish origin and the signs and language spoken were mostly Spanish. Just by the side of the square was a large Romanesque cathedral, the stones bleached white by centuries of sunshine. They found a bodega where men and women were eating.

"It's lovely. I never knew that it existed."

"Our set never goes farther than the Carlton. It's our island. But Mallacca has its natives. We only see them in banks or in the hotels."

He opened the car door for her and everyone in the bar strained their necks to look at them; a group of children surrounded the car, regarding it with amazement.

The owner of the bodega, bowing awkwardly, served them. Fritz ordered some langoustines, cold chicken, a thick slab of chorizo, some tomatoes and two bottles of cold white wine. He spoke Spanish as fluently as English and German, having lived in Madrid during the war with his aunts, and the owner looked surprised and pleased by his linguistic ability. He wished them *buen provecho*.

Fritz counted the children surrounding the car—eleven—and he ordered ice cream for all of them. When Fritz and Maureen pulled away from the bodega they could hear the thin small voices of the children cheering them.

The beach was located a quarter of a mile beyond the village and Fritz drove onto the sand. He pulled out the large paper bag and Maureen carried the wine.

"Shall we have a swim first?" she asked.

"Yes, whatever you like."

She began taking her clothes off and he turned away.

"You can look if you can bear it," she said. He still averted his eyes. "You're shy, really, aren't you?"

"Not usually," he said. "It's just that I haven't been with anyone I cared about since I was a boy and I feel rather intimidated."

She turned him around. He was still wearing trousers and tennis shoes. She placed her arms around his neck.

"My breasts are small but my heart is big." She kissed him on the mouth and he was overcome by a wave of tenderness.

He was surprised by the anxiety he felt. After all wasn't she just another girl?

"You know, Maureen, I'm not going to give you up," he said.

CHAPTER 8

The Grande Casino occupied a wedge-shaped block at the end of the Coronet Walk. Signs posted throughout the town directed tourists to the Casino. The building, a white alabaster monstrosity, had been erected by a group of Corsicans at the turn of the century. They had hoped to make Mallacca another Baden or Monte Carlo, but the island's citizens were too poor to gamble and those foreigners in search of a holiday preferred Nice. The Corsicans had declared themselves bankrupt and fled.

For years the building remained shuttered until the present Count decided to reopen it in the late fifties. But Paul Martell, after an extensive and expensive publicity campaign to attract the international gambling set, had fared no better than the Corsicans. It was with considerable relief that he passed on the lease to Archimedes Pendelos in 1964. Paul thought with amusement that for once Arki had outsmarted himself. But to his shock and embarrassment, the Casino under Arki's direction had prospered, for Arki had been able to attract all the international gamblers who had grown tired of Las Vegas and the south of France. An opportunity to gamble, even by proxy, against Archimedes, was a challenge that no one could resist.

When Arki's party entered the Casino, heads turned, croupiers let their eyes wander from the tables, and for a second there was silence, for the king had come to inspect one of his provinces. Breitner, Arki's aide, had come along for a discreet look at the books.

"Get some chips for my guests," Arki instructed him.

"How many, Mr. Pendelos?"

Nick had already taken out some cash when Arki waved his hand commandingly.

"You can do that at Cannes or Monte Carlo but not here."

"I'd prefer to play with my own money," Nick said forthrightly. He was a sponger but what endeared him to everyone was that he never behaved like one.

"A thousand for everyone," Arki said. "If you win, you can return the house's chips. How's that?"

"How can we refuse those odds?" Deborah said. "Arki's got the house advantage to start with. Are we going to play roulette, Toni?"

"In a few minutes. Why don't you start?"

As Deborah moved off to the roulette table and Nick to chemin de fer, Toni looked around the room. No loudmouthed crapshooters or bunnies dealing blackjack, thank God. A horseshoe bar in tasteful mahogany with a white ivory top served as a rendezvous for the local *poules*, but even they were well dressed in fashionable sheathlike gowns and they blended in with the surroundings. Paul had allowed common streetwalkers in, but Arki had put a stop to that.

Arki came up to her and he held his new watch to her ear.

"We've been engaged for twenty-three hours, nineteen minutes."

He took her hand and held it tightly and she could feel his knuckles pressing against her thigh as they walked to the table. A croupier brought over two chairs for them and Toni placed some money on black (Arki's color, she thought) and also double zero. Across the table from them, Deborah sat with a young man foppishly dressed in a black velvet suit.

"We're on a winning streak, Arki," Deborah said with an air of defiance.

"Treize, noir et impair," the croupier announced as the wheel slowed.

"That's us," Brian shouted.

"Do you know my sister, Toni, and Archimedes Pendelos?" Deborah asked.

"No, haven't had the pleasure," Brian replied.

"This is Brian Teal," Deborah said, making the introductions. "And God, is he lucky. I've finally met a winner."

Madeleine arched her back on the chaise longue. The lights were on in the swimming pool, and she was tempted to go in for a swim. The script conference hadn't gone well with Ricardo. He was suspicious, stubborn, and as fretful as a child in the care of a stranger. They had first gone for a drive and had then had dinner. Even with the help of a delicious Chablis, the meal was not a success.

Madeleine had kept up a steady stream of conversation on the worthlessness of directors, the lack of good scripts, the failure of studio publicity departments, all of which Ricardo had barely listened to. She had failed to make one sensible suggestion about the script they were committed to, and Ricardo from time to time had let his mind wander. He pictured Carla fretting and furious, spending an insufferable evening with Giovanni. He knew too that she'd make him pay for his decision to accept the film. But he had no alternative.

Now, sitting by the pool, he lost his sense of reality. What was he doing there at ten o'clock at night with Madeleine who was discoursing on Fritz's failure as a husband.

"You've never lived in Germany, have you?"

"No, but I don't see what this has to do with our discussion." The sultry night air made him perspire freely and he was extremely uncomfortable. "Can I turn off the lights? They're attracting all the insects in Mallacca."

"Insects, hah. Germans, they're the real insects. Fritz lives for one thing—his work. But all Germans are alike in that respect. They want to fill their stomachs, guzzle beer, work fourteen hours a day and poke their wives twenty-seven times a month. Thank God, nature has found a way of giving a woman a few days of freedom. Everything is a schedule. Before computers there were Germans, programming their existence. Fritz's idea of a good time is visiting hydroelectric plants or touring his atomic stockpile. Then he relaxes in the evening by going over financial reports with Wagner blaring in the background. Is it any wonder that the French and Italians have always despised the Germans?"

"That's not quite true," he observed.

"Oh, you mean the military side. Well, military men of all nations are the same, so of course alliances have been formed with Germany."

"It doesn't seem to me that Fritz fits into the pattern. I've always thought him to be extremely civilized and intelligent."

"You've never been to bed with him."

"Well, of course I haven't."

"He's indifferent . . ." Suddenly, she unbuttoned the front of her dress to reveal the fact that she wore nothing underneath. "Can you imagine turning your back on this?" she demanded furiously. "Men would kill for me."

Ricardo turned his head away.

"Why are you hiding?" She dropped the dress and stood in front of him like the Playmate-of-the-Month. "Come on, let's go for a swim. It's absolutely impossible to breathe in this humidity."

"I think it would be better if I waited in the villa for you."

"Don't be such a child . . . the sweat's pouring off you. Have a swim, you'll feel revived."

Before he could restrain her, she had torn open his shirt and was unloosening his belt. He resisted clumsily, pulling away from her, but she held tightly to his neck and rubbed her body against him.

"Don't be shy, Ricardo. We are going to work together. Co-stars have to get to know one another in order to work together effectively."

"This isn't in my contract."

"It's a bonus, *chéri.*" She unzipped his fly and his trousers dropped down; he fell into a chair. She pulled off his loafers and then his trousers.

"I think you're insane, Madeleine."

"Am I? Is Carla insane also? I've wondered for years what she saw in you and I want to find out. Are you afraid of me?"

He sat on the canvas chair looking disconsolately at his trousers twisted up on the blue mosaic squares, and for a moment he thought that this was a guilty, fearful dream, a form of penance he must pay to Giovanni. He looked up and saw Madeleine's face before him, the lips slightly parted, and the soft creamy texture of her body. Her face, so close to his, appeared gigantic.

She sat across his knees like a little girl waiting to be petted. She touched his thigh with her nails and he felt a chill of ex-pectation. Impossible to explain to this virago, he thought, that he was in love with Carla. Their relationship was based on trust, and although they had both had innumerable opportunities to have affairs, meaningless in the long run, they had withstood the temptations offered by their position and profession. It was in a sense a marriage, a love affair in which both partners were perfectly requited. But this would be beyond the grasp of Madeleine. He tried to push her off, but she tightened her grip around him and became more passionate as he resisted.

"I've always wanted you, Ricardo. I've seen your dreadful

films with Carla and when I think of them I always see myself
playing Carla's role."

"I can't believe you're serious . . . and there's nothing between
Carla and me except professional respect. We work well together."

"Darling, you're talking to Madeleine. You've both been careful and resourceful but don't you think that people know about
the two of you?"

She placed his hand between her bare thighs and moved back
and forth rhythmically. She moved her breasts against his mouth.
He turned his head away and made an effort to move her off
him, but she refused to give way.

He felt his excitement mount despite himself. Finally, breath-
lessly, he moved his mouth over her breasts and she squeezed
the back of his head until it hurt. His tongue was hot and dry
and it grew moist as he ran it over her nipples.

She pulled his striped undershorts from beneath her and
slipped over his bare thighs. Her legs were on top of the arm-
rests and she held the metal prongs supporting them and swayed
back and forth like a child on a swing. She raised and lowered
her body with the grace and balance of a gymnast, until she
felt herself going weak as she reached a climax.

"My darling Ricardo . . ." She lost her voice and continued
to move over his thighs. He suddenly stiffened and groaned
and she realized that what could have been a disaster had
turned into a victory.

They lay on a beach towel together, like exhausted children
who had just completed a race. He turned his back on her. He
was disgusted by his weakness.

I have betrayed Carla and it will never again be the same, he
thought bitterly. He had destroyed the illusion of happiness and
with it part of himself.

Carla stood on the balcony overlooking the Coronet Walk,
hoping to recognize the Chrysler convertible that Madeleine

and Ricardo had left in. It was almost midnight and they had gone off right after lunch. Where were they? Nine hours with Madeleine! She almost choked on the name. And yet in the old days before the two women had become international stars, they had been friends, they'd shared a small room at the Villa Roso, eaten at the same bars, fought off the same American stars and producers who wanted the newest starlets to help them relax. There had been a true camaraderie. Whoever worked paid for meals and the rent. Madeleine had been trustworthy, someone who treated confidences with respect and was there when she was needed.

And where would Madeleine be now if Carla hadn't been her friend that time of Madeleine's trouble?

The Villa Roso lay behind the Spanish Steps on a crooked little street called Via Alphonso. Next door to the hotel was the Café Roma where the two took most of their meals unless they could find a man who wanted nothing more than company and then there would be dinner at the Fiorenze or the Excelsior. On the bus back from Cinecittà that day Carla had noticed that Madeleine was unusually silent and preoccupied. Madeleine sat sullenly looking out of the window, and Carla refrained from talking until she saw that her friend was crying. She reached over and grasped Madeleine's hand. Madeleine leaned her head on Carla's shoulder, and her body shook with anguish she could not control.

"Tell me, Madeleine. Come on, it can't be so bad. You didn't get the part in the Metro film?"

"I got it, that's just the point. And I've accepted." She now began to sob hysterically. "But I can't do it."

"For God's sake, why? They pay good money, don't they? And you got it on your own, so there's no agent's commission."

Madeleine sat up stiffly and released Carla's hand. She tried to open the window because the heat in the bus was stifling, but it remained stuck. Carla stood up and pressed down both metal buttons and with a tremendous heave managed to jar it open.

The humid sticky air blew in, but it was better than simply sweltering. Carla felt faint after sitting down. The temperature had soared into the nineties and everyone who had to be in Rome suffered and complained.

"Don't you want to tell me about it? After all you should be dancing. How much are they going to pay you?"

"Three hundred American dollars for a week's work."

"Madeleine, you're rich." Carla calculated the enormous sum in lire. "Why that's two hundred and ten thousand lire! You can live like a queen for two months. When do you start?"

"I'm not going to do it. I can't, I can't!" she stormed.

"It's not *cinéma bleu?*" They both had had many offers to do pornographic films and had refused various overtures from Scandinavian and German organizations who recruited girls in Rome. "No, of course it's legitimate. It's Metro. Silly me . . ."

They rode in silence until they reached the stop at the Spanish Steps. The driver shouted *"Ciao, bellezzas"* as he did every afternoon and tried to pinch their bottoms and got his hand slapped. It was a standing joke and occasionally to his shock they let him pinch when they didn't have the fare. This afternoon they had paid and no feelies were offered. They walked past the Spanish Steps, ignoring the usual mob of tourists snapping photographs of Rome's unemployed beautiful people who used the Steps as a meeting place.

"Let's have a coffee at the Roma," Carla suggested. "It will make you feel better and Luigi has two large fans working now. We can cool off."

They waved to the crowd of paparazzi who sat on the terrace of the Roma. It was too early to catch anyone behaving indiscreetly. Mario, a tall, slender photographer who always managed to get his clothes at Brioni's, stood up and offered them a seat at his table. No one quite knew how he got his money. It was rumored that he was involved with a Mafia Capo and that he had a blackmail business.

"Some day, you'll both come to me on your knees," he taunted them.

"We'll let you know by carrier pigeon," Carla replied.

As they passed inside, Luigi signaled them to a table. The waiter brought them two cappuccinos sprinkled with chocolate flakes. Madeleine had been composed since leaving the bus, and Carla decided not to press her. Several girls they knew and worked with called greetings to them.

"My one chance . . . *Merde . . . Ma vie est terminée . . . c'est affreux . . .*" Madeleine broke off.

"You are twenty and incredibly beautiful and your life is over? How is it over?"

"*Je suis enceinte. Enceinte!*"

Carla dropped her coffee cup and its contents splattered over her thin white cotton dress.

"Damn, look what I've done. Did I hit you as well?"

"Did you hear what I said?" Madeleine insisted.

"Yes, I heard. And listen to me, you're talking complete nonsense. This isn't the first time a girl got into some trouble."

"Trouble! It's more than that. I asked the man responsible to help me, and of course he's married and he told me he'd call the police, get my permit revoked and prosecute me for blackmail. How do you like that?"

"Who is it? Maybe I can go to see him."

"Carlucci, the head of the union at Cinecittà. Oh, God, it was so stupid. He asked me out for a date about three months ago and we went to an Albergo in the hills and it was all amusing and . . . I had too much to drink. On the way back we parked by the reservoir and I think I blacked out . . . I was so dizzy. And when I opened my eyes he was making love to me and I knew I couldn't stop him. It didn't seem to matter. When I got back to Villa Roso you were sleeping and I passed out. The next morning my head ached but I had no distinct recollection of what had happened. I thought perhaps I dreamed it all, and I'd look like an idiot accusing him when I saw him . . . and of course he's important and could get me barred from the studio . . . so I did nothing. I just avoided him as you do someone you have a bad feeling about."

"You're certain that you're not just late?"

"This is the third month I've been late. I thought maybe the heat made me irregular. It happened to me several years ago and I didn't think anything of it. Haven't you noticed the way I've been eating and my figure . . . my brassieres don't fit any more and when I wear a girdle I start to feel faint."

Carla thought over the situation for a few minutes in silence.

"I know what you are thinking," Madeleine said. "An abortion. It's the only way, but Carla, I'm afraid, and you know I'm not afraid of anything."

"I know that. You've more courage than I've ever had."

"If I put myself into the hands of one of those butchers behind Via Veneto I'll wind up in the morgue or floating in the canal. That's what they do to the girls when it's gone badly. And as for the Metro film, I'll have to tell them I can't do it . . . and I'll never be asked again. This was a chance but I can't stand the heat and the lights and it's one of those battle scenes which require twenty or thirty takes." She nervously pushed her long blond hair out of her eyes.

"Listen, I've heard of a man who does abortions. He's a doctor at the medical school. Professor Guardo, that's his name. One of the girls at the studio went to him at his clinic and he did it, and she was all right afterward. In just a week she'd recovered and since then she had a baby, so he must know what he's doing. Look, I'll call her now. She'll give me the information. What do you say?"

"You could try, I suppose," Madeleine said despondently.

"Cheer up. Your friend Carla won't let anything happen to you."

Carla returned in five minutes. She was sweating profusely from the heat in the telephone booth which she had been forced to keep closed.

"It's hopeless, isn't it?"

"Not hopeless. But expensive. She can contact him for you and make all the arrangements." She paused, looked at Madeleine's blue eyes. "Three hundred thousand lire to be paid in advance."

"Hopeless, I told you, didn't I?"

The two left the Roma at seven o'clock and Madeleine complained of a terrible headache and decided to return to the Villa Roso, have a bath and try to go to sleep. Carla walked aimlessly down the Via Veneto, desperately attempting to puzzle out a solution. Nothing short of selling herself to the highest bidder could raise that much money. And even then, how much would a man pay for an evening with a woman? She found herself back at the Café Roma and this time when she saw Mario playing with his Nikon she went over without an invitation and sat down opposite him.

"My lucky day. Little did I realize when I woke up this morning that Carla Fabrizzi would simply sit down at my table without having to be persuaded with a Beretta."

"You always make such flowery speeches, Mario. Do you ever mean anything you say?"

"To you I never fail to tell the truth." He took out a comb and ran it through his slick black hair, then waved the comb at a waiter. "What will you have, Carla? Dinner? I'm prepared to be extravagant to a fault for you."

"Just coffee, please," she said, looking away from the regulars who noticed her joining Mario and had begun to gossip.

The night air was heavy and lay like an immovable blanket over her. She ruffled the white collar of her dress which was sticking to her neck. She would have given anything for a cool bath and an air-conditioned room with crisp, fresh sheets on the bed. Mario almost read her thoughts.

"Wouldn't dinner and dancing at the Excelsior be pleasant?"

"Pleasant if you had a hundred thousand lire to throw into the street. And even if you could afford it, I haven't got a decent dress to wear. I'd look a fool."

"You're dressed perfectly for any occasion, Carla. Men are interested in what a girl looks like, not who her dressmaker is."

"Have you any plans for this evening or are you going to remain at the Roma?" Carla asked.

He made an effort to appear languid as he peered at his platinum-banded wristwatch.

"I have a meeting at ten thirty with some business associates, but that won't take long. You can have me all to yourself afterward if you like."

"You make yourself sound so important."

"Do you doubt that I am? I earn good money, wear the best clothes, eat where I choose and have a new Fiat 1500. And of course," he added after a moment, "a new apartment at the Via Veneto Palazzo. You don't get those things without money and connections."

He was, she knew, telling the truth. He spent a considerable amount simply to maintain a front. He also appeared to know all sorts of people. At various times she had seen film producers and bankers join him for a drink, and once one of her friends had pointed out a man with him who was reputed to be the head of the most important advertising agency in Rome. Despite his bluff manner and his air of self-importance, Mario did have influential friends. She wondered if she ought to tell him about Madeleine's problem. No, that wouldn't serve any purpose. He only did favors when it could be useful to him.

"Little short of rent this month?" he asked, sitting back on his chair so that only the back legs touched the ground.

"No, why? Did you hear that I was?"

"I hear a great many things, most of them lies. But I sift out the lies from the truth. I simply wondered why tonight you decided to join me. My efforts haven't been as futile as I thought."

"You try too hard. Sometimes a simple approach is the best one."

He snapped his fingers for the waiter, handed him a twenty thousand lire note with an air of indifference and stood up with a great flourish. He dangled the camera strap around his wrist, and she lost her self-control, feeling herself flush with panic.

"Mario, do you have to leave right now?"

"I've offered you dinner and you've declined, so like a good businessman I cut my losses before they become painful or damaging." He gave her a courtly bow and started for the red Fiat parked at the curb. It gleamed like a mirror. She followed him to the car. "Have you decided to reconsider?" He tapped his shoe against the curb, inserted a toothpick in the corner of his mouth, and closed his eyes for a moment.

The saliva left her mouth as she tried to talk.

"Mario . . . just a minute more . . . please."

"Yes, all right." He opened his eyes and removed the toothpick from his mouth. "Well, I'm waiting. My time isn't without value."

She was never certain how she managed to force the words out.

"Mario, I need money . . . a lot of money."

"Don't we all? Not so easy to live from day to day. I should know. Before reaching my present standards I was not unlike most of the layabouts you see at the Roma. In fact one of the reasons I still come here is to remind myself that I'm one of the fortunate few who've escaped."

"Can you help me?"

"I suppose you need it in a hurry. Well, get in. You can ride with me up to the Fiorenze."

The car smelled clean and fresh, and the upholstery, she realized, was real leather. She'd never been in such a luxurious car.

"Like it? It has a souped-up engine and will do two hundred kilometers an hour when I've broken it in."

"It's very impressive. It must've cost you a fortune."

"I can afford it. In fact, just to be on the safe side, I keep it at a private garage near my apartment. Those boys who roam the streets at night have no respect for private property."

She couldn't tell him about Madeleine because that would make her friend vulnerable as well.

"It's my mother. She must have an operation and we haven't the money to pay for it."

"That's sad. One must do what one can for one's parents. You have a good heart."

"The operation can only be done in Rome by a specialist and it's very expensive."

"I don't suppose she has private medical insurance . . . no, she wouldn't. Well, how can I be of assistance, Carla?"

"I need four hundred thousand lire for the surgeon and hospital," she said anxiously.

"That's quite a sum . . . but not impossible to earn over a . . . well, for you as an extra I think perhaps two or three years, provided you're careful and thrifty. But I don't imagine your mother can hold out for that long, can she?"

"This week—I need it this week. The surgeon is booked months in advance and he can only fit her in now. I've got to have the money."

"Well, we'd all like to have four hundred thousand lire whenever we require it. But some of us have to work for it. We simply can't ask people for a sum like that without giving something in return."

"I don't care what I have to do." She felt tremendously relieved now that she had committed herself. That was the worst part—offering yourself. Once you made up your mind, it was easier. They stopped for a light by the side of the Colosseum, and Mario turned to her. His sallow skin appeared even darker under the street lamps. He reached over and put his hand on her thigh. His breath smelled of the licorice breath tablets that he constantly chewed. His hand glided up her thigh and she became nervous and flustered.

"The light's changed. What do you say? Can you help me?"

"I might be able to." She eased her head back on the cool leather headrest as he started off. "You might have to do a few things that could upset you but if you're prepared to do as I tell you"—he stopped and smiled—"well, nothing is impossible for a beautiful girl who isn't afraid. After all, we have a duty toward our parents and our mothers are sacred."

She couldn't talk. She closed her eyes and nodded dumbly. Other girls lived with these things, blotted them out of their minds once they were married or launched on successful careers.

The car park of the Fiorenze was packed and the attendant waved Mario away with his flashlight. But Mario pulled up under the red-striped canopy.

"Oh, it's you, Mario," the attendant said deferentially.

"Thought I was a tourist, eh? What a business."

Mario paused inside by the crowded bar and steered Carla toward a barman who waved at him.

"Give her what she likes," he said.

"I feel so out of place . . . look at the furs and jewelry of these women."

"They'd gladly exchange everything to look like you. I will have to have my meeting now, then I'll be back for you. Be sure you've carefully thought over what I told you. The implications . . ."

"I've made up my mind, Mario," she said as he released her hand.

"Good. I'll see what I can do to help you with your problem."

She ordered the mildest drink she could think of, sweet sherry on the rocks. A plate of hot tidbits was placed in front of her by the barman who seemed anxious to please. Obviously Mario tipped him well. After draining half her drink she felt more relaxed. The air-conditioning made a tremendous difference; people could breathe, move about, dance to the smooth Latin orchestra playing in the central dining room. She noticed several men glance in her direction. They all were cut from the same mold—dark mohair suits, white or beige silk ties; stocky and middle-aged with wire-rimmed, pale yellow glasses; they were accompanied by heavyset women gabbling among themselves. The women all wore black dresses, large diamond rings and clips, with mink wraps around their shoulders. They might have belonged to some club. But this was the way the Roman middle class looked—not an aristocrat among them; all solid, solvent, thick-skinned citizens in a society of material well-being.

She could never become part of this class. Either she would fall into the gutter, sinking to the level of the common street-walker, or soar above it all and find her place in Roman society. No middle ground for Carla. Nervously, she drained her glass, observed the women peering curiously at her. One day, she thought, I will make you all sorry that you were born. Your husbands will force you to see my films, they will stare at my photographs in the newspapers and magazines and have secret fantasies about me.

She changed to gin and bitter lemon and immediately had a sensation of mild elation. Gin was quick and effective. Oh, yes, much better for making you dizzy and indifferent. She closed her eyes and visualized Madeleine's sad little face.

Mario returned to the bar by himself, but she saw three other men waiting near the doorway and smiling in her direction. They were all fair-haired and light-skinned. One had a blond beard and bright blue eyes.

"Well, did you have a drink?"

"Yes . . . I've mixed and feel a bit peculiar. But the gin was rather nice."

Mario signaled for the bill and with a great flourish signed it. Somehow the grand manner suited him. It had never occurred to her, seeing him at the Roma, that he was anything more than a third-rate operator, always searching for an angle.

"I've got bottles of gin at my place," he said.

"Are we going with those men at the door?"

"Yes, they're business associates. I think I've found a way to help you." Her face tightened. "Come on, cheer up. Everything will work out . . . after all, it's in a worthy cause."

She was too frightened to speak on the short ride to the center of Rome, and sat stupefied. A doorman at the Veneto Palazzo opened the door for her and took Mario's car. The block had white marble pillars in the Ionic style and a portico running around the entire building. The main hallway had a porter's desk, with mailboxes and a switchboard behind it.

"Any messages, Antonio?" Mario asked.

"*Si*, signor." He handed two slips of paper to Mario, who glanced at them and crumpled them.

"Nothing important," he said, leading Carla to the lift, where an attendant in a blue and white uniform bowed and bid them good evening. They stopped at twenty, and the attendant opened the door, and again bowed. Carla stared at him, unaccustomed to such service. She followed Mario down the corridor, and her heels sank into the deep-pile green carpet. Even the hallway was air-conditioned.

"Here we are, Carla," he said, ushering her into a large, L-shaped living room, elegantly furnished with contemporary Scandinavian furniture. She liked the blond deal side-tables and the stereo enclosed in a teak cabinet. There was even a television set.

"Come out on the balcony and you'll see the view."

Outside the air was heavy and oppressive.

"My God, you've got all of Rome," she said excitedly. "I've never seen anything like this outside of a film. And it's all yours. I never realized that a photographer could earn so much."

"Photographer," he chuckled. "Who said I was a photographer?"

"You're always carrying a camera, so I thought—I am silly."

"I take photos as a hobby. I'm a broker, but I don't deal in stocks and shares. The word is used in an unconventional sense. Let me give you an example. If you want a car and the dealer can't get you delivery for a few months and you come to me, I get one for you immediately. I have connections in Torino and for a service charge the car is yours. If you want to meet a producer or an advertising agency executive, or you want your name in the newspapers or what else?" He placed a finger thoughtfully against his temple. "If you have a desire, I can see that it is fulfilled, provided you pay my commission. I'm a human broker who provides a service. Let us say you have a business and you need a loan and the banks won't help, well, I can arrange the finance. Or you want to build a house or block of apartments and need permission from the authorities and they won't give it, I then go to work and see that the proper licenses are secured."

"It sounds fascinating," she admitted. "But how do you fix your commission?"

"Good question. Obviously it all depends on the value to the individual. Sometimes seventy-five percent or twenty-five percent. I use my best judgment and I always get a retainer, just to show good faith."

"I'm not in a position to pay you a retainer."

"I know that," he replied with a twinkle in his eyes, "but others can."

"Those men I saw at the Fiorenze . . ."

She bit her lip anxiously and couldn't bring herself to probe any further. Mario looked at his watch, then led her back into the living room, put some music on the stereo and pointed to a dressing room with a bathroom.

"Why don't you go in and freshen up. You'll find some costumes in the wardrobe. Try the nurse's outfit. I think it will fit you."

She nodded and went into the room. In the wardrobe she saw dozens of costumes: a nun's habit, a circus clown's, beaded evening gowns, prison uniforms. It was almost like the wardrobe at the studio. She ran some water and took off her dress. She stood looking at her figure in the full-length mirror, then removed her bra and panties and sat in the warm bath. A hand reached through the door and she was startled.

"It's only me," Mario said, without coming in. "I've mixed a gin and tonic for you." She took the drink, thanking him weakly, and drank it in the bath. As she bathed, she heard the doorbell and then voices and greetings.

The uniform was snow-white and starched and looked like

one that detergent commercials featured; she slipped into it, crossing the straps across her shoulders and buttoning up the back. There was also a small cap which she pinned to her hair, as she'd seen in the movies.

When she came back into the living room she was surprised to see only Mario there.

"Pretty as a picture. The uniform really suits you."

"I thought I heard voices," she said, trembling.

"My associates are in the other room. My, you are an actress. You actually seem nervous. That's very good. My only instructions to you are to seem tense and frightened when you go in to meet them. They like the appearance of innocence."

"When do I get paid?"

"Half now and half when you've completed your work." He fished out two hundred thousand lire and she stuffed them into a secret compartment in her handbag. "Don't worry, no one's going to touch your bag," he said, noticing her hesitate.

"What . . . I'm . . . don't know . . ." she whispered incoherently. The room was suddenly circling around and she leaned against the wall for support.

"Did the drink go to your head?"

"I think . . . no . . . no, I'll be all right. Just butterflies."

He opened the door to another room bathed in bright light which blinded her. She could just make out the outlines of figures. A hand shoved her forward and she thought she would fall, but strong hairy arms supported her; then before she knew what was happening another man seized her just under the arm and she felt herself pulled to an even brighter section right in the glare of the lights. A man's beard was close to her face, and a wet pink mouth was all over her neck. She tried to push the face away, but another, stronger pair of hands pushed her down and she found herself lying on a bed. She started to scream and a black gag was tightly secured to her mouth. They were going to murder her! She struggled with the gag, but her arms were pinned behind her and strapped to the bedpost. Her legs kicked out, but it was no use. They were strong. How many were there?

She tried to think clearly but she couldn't imagine what was going on. Her white uniform was torn open, and then she felt her underclothes being ripped off. She groaned in pain as a man forced her thighs apart. They were like beasts all over her. She heard a whirring noise that sounded familiar. Gasping and struggling, she was pushed over on her side and a man shoved hard into her backside and she writhed in agony.

It was all going black and she fought to hold on to the thread of consciousness. Her gag was dropped and she started to scream, but a pair of hands forced her jaws apart and she couldn't control the muscles of her mouth which locked in a spasm. Then a man forced himself into her mouth and she felt herself choking. It seemed to be going on for hours.

There were three of them and they took turns; then mercifully she blacked out. The room was in darkness when she awoke. Her body was sore and she could barely move her mouth. She touched something soft at the edge of the bed and recoiled when she saw that it was the long head of a rubber snake. The eyes and tongue were so real that she jumped away and began to shriek. A lamp was switched on, and she saw that she was in a bedroom. Mario stood at the foot of the bed.

"You were very good, Carla. Here's the rest of your money. Any time you want some help—"

"Help? You're all animals!"

"These Swedes are energetic, aren't they?"

"Why didn't you tell me?"

"The element of surprise is essential to a film of this kind. If you tell a girl what's going to take place she starts to enjoy it. This group wanted a film of an actual rape, and they went away well satisfied."

She wandered the streets for hours. At midday she found herself at the Café Roma. In the ladies' room she stared at her face in the mirror. There was no difference. Her body ached and her muscles were tensed, but that was all. She made a vow to blot out the experience. "It never happened," she said aloud.

When she came out, she found Madeleine sitting at her table.

"Luigi said you'd come in."

"How do you feel?" Carla asked.

"This morning I had some nausea, but now I'm all right. You didn't come in last night."

"No, I didn't. I went to see a friend and look"—she opened her bag and showed Madeleine the money—"I persuaded him to loan me the money, so you'll be all right."

"Oh, Carla, I can't believe it. No one's ever had a friend like you."

As Carla stood watching the blinking lights of boats in the bay below her balcony, it all seemed light-years ago. But now Madeleine had come into her life again and was threatening to destroy it. She was startled to hear Giovanni's voice behind her.

"Aren't you coming to bed, Carla?"

"In a minute," she replied lifelessly.

"What do you find so interesting out there at this time?"

"I was simply thinking of how far I've come and what a short fall it is into the street below."

"I'll never let you fall," he said, taking her hand and rubbing it over his lips. "You see, Carla, it's all right for Madeleine to do the rubbish—she never had any talent—but you're an artist with God-given talent, and I'm the shepherd of it, so I have a great responsibility. Working with Ricardo has become a pleasant habit, and of course it was profitable, but you have more than that and I want you to use that talent . . . to extend it. You'll play Petrarch's Laura in your next film and we'll get a real actor to play opposite you."

She sat on her bed and Giovanni removed her furry slippers and kissed her feet.

"Darling, I worship you . . . and I'm not going to play games with a ham actor who only wants to further his career at your expense."

Was that all it had been for Ricardo? An obvious formula of exploitation that required no great ingenuity? Just make the leading lady fall in love with you. Giovanni embraced her, and although his touch was momentarily strange, she went limp in his arms, victimized by his passion and grateful for what he had given her. Respect was not easily available on the open market, no matter how much you were prepared to pay.

The sea was unexpectedly rough and the tender pitched and truckled waywardly on the short run back to the *Archimedes*. Gavin held onto a metal bar in the stern seat and swallowed the bile welling up in the back of his throat. Vomiting now would spoil an otherwise perfect day, one of the happiest he'd had in years. Mulholland had dozed off in the leather stool next to the control panel and his head wagged forward painlessly. The third member of the shore party, Tommy Ambrose-Smith, stood several feet from Gavin, nervously having a private conversation with himself. The story he had prepared for Victoria was so complicated and farfetched that he himself had difficulty keeping the facts straight. If only he could get through the night without an inquisition he'd be better prepared after a good night's sleep to deal with his wife in the morning.

The tender driver reversed his engines as he edged alongside the boat. Several seamen secured the ropes to the side, and the three men climbed up the wooden ladder and walked along the dimly lit deck. According to the first mate a party led by Toni and Arki had gone ashore for dinner some hours earlier. He was somewhat vague about whether Victoria had been with them, and Tommy decided not to press him. The three said quiet good nights and Tommy headed for his room which was next to the salon on the deck below. He hesitated outside, trying to catch a sound. If Victoria was in, surely there would be a noise—her heavy cigarette cough or the swish of a dressing gown. Slowly, his tension mounting, he turned the knob and to his relief found the cabin empty. A few dresses were hanging out and he rooted around for a note. Nothing. She probably got tired of waiting and swept her suspicions under the carpet as she usually did. After all, he'd been with John and Gavin—they'd swear for him. But was the word of either enough to convince Victoria if testimony was required and demanded?

He had a raw taste in his mouth compounded of cigarettes, too much whiskey, and an empty, acidic stomach. Also there was the lingering memory of the young Italian boy with the shock of twisted curls crowning his head like a black olive wreath. He'd been inexperienced but willing and curiously frightened, and Tommy could not conquer the serpentine fear that it had all been a bit of an act. Like most people who required a great deal of sex, Tommy was unable to attribute anything beyond his own motives to the partners he picked up for an evening. And yet, there'd been something about the boy. A kind of quiet innocence that he hadn't encountered in years.

In London, Tommy's set was made up of aging, malicious men who behaved as if they were still the fretful public-school boys they had once been. Simply a queer drunken crowd of chums who insisted on the preeminence of class ties. He'd given out a dozen keys to the house in Putney, and now when he wanted to use it for a few hours he had to make arrangements with as many people, to be sure that the more vicious Teddy Boys who had found favor with his friends weren't going to be brought down for the afternoon.

In spite of the care he took to guard his secret Tommy had been blackmailed twice. The change of laws the year before had been intended for the anonymous thousands who practiced in lonely room and bars and were subjected to the hounding of the English policeman. But what happened to you if you were in the limelight and married to a duchess whose relationship to the throne was uncomfortably close? You lived your life as though it were some cautionary tale for the benefit of a schoolboy's edification. People survived financial disaster, the church's displeasure, the confessional's fall from grace for venal sins, but no one in England had ever survived scandal and no one ever would so long as a social hierarchy existed.

He slipped off his clothes and piled them on the curved sofa facing the bed. As he pushed open the bathroom door he recoiled, startled. Sitting on the bath stool was a ghostly figure in a white robe. He switched on the light.

"Turn it off, for God's sake," Victoria said. "It hurts my eyes."

"What're you doing in there?" he asked, then flustering, he switched off the light.

"I've been waiting . . . for you," she replied in a low voice that controlled and modulated emotion perfectly. It had spoken in public thousands of times at the launching of ships in Southampton, at cornerstone layings in Hammersmith, at hospitals and at trade fairs throughout the world, and it had the heavy melody that comes from years of public practice and professional enthusiasm.

"I thought you'd gone ashore with the rest of the party."

"I decided not to. I'm tired of imposing on other men or behaving like a new widow."

"Do you have to get so melodramatic? We all had a few too many and got involved with some people Gavin knew from the States."

"For a change I'd prefer the truth."

"You just heard it. Now if you don't mind I'd like to shower if I may."

She got up from the stool and let him pass and went into the bedroom.

"I know what you are, what you do, but can't you from time to time avoid humiliating me in front of my friends?" She sighed heavily, shifted over Tommy's clothes and sank into the sofa. "You're a grown man, not a child."

"Meaning?" He switched on the water to cut off her reply.

"Meaning," she said in a tired, resigned voice, "that you indulge yourself. If you weren't married, you could do as you like. Aren't you conscious of any responsibility toward me?"

"Your good name and reputation, Ma'am, are the albatross I

wear in public every day of my life. I want a life as well and I'm going to have one."

"Have I ever denied you your rights? Most of the time I'm looking the other way—not in the direction of Putney."

He almost slipped on the tile. Obviously he hadn't been as discreet as he'd thought and now the consequences confronted him with the inevitability of a New Year's Day hangover. Well, he consoled himself, he'd made the effort. There was that to be said in his favor.

"You're most pathetic when you're determined to deceive me. I'm thirty-eight and for most of those years I've lived on the covers of magazines in badly reproduced photographs; my small talk, which is at best uninteresting, has appeared in articles and gossip columns; my choice of clothes has been the subject of controversy as meaningless and banal as most of my activities. But I fell in love with you while all my faculties functioned—no midsummer madness for me—and I knew perfectly well that you were a man of small talent, mean spirit and ungenerous to a fault, yet the fact remained that I wanted you to marry me. Children might have affected you in some way, but I rather think not."

He stood listening, watching the pearly globules of water spitting from the shower head. All of it was true and he made no protest, for he prided himself on the absence of hypocrisy which he thought redeemed his other faults.

"Have you a constructive suggestion?" he asked, certain that she had none.

"Divorce," she said simply.

"Divorce?" The one action he counted on her to avoid. Ridiculous idea. He couldn't entertain it for a moment, for it meant giving up the comfortable Wilshire estate, the Belgrave Square palace, the servants, the comfortable allowance, the contacts that made up the small change of his daily existence. He was prepared to forsake anything except celebrity.

"Don't push too hard too fast," he said weakly.

"I can live with the gutter press; the question is, can you? You've reminded me dozens of times that I've robbed you of your manhood and your chosen profession. I hate to think of myself destroying you. If you want to go back to designing sets in tatty rep companies and shopping for wallpaper with old ladies, and fighting tooth and nail for your little commissions, I won't stand in your way. I'm a patron of the arts and I refuse to smother talent, no matter how slender," she said, lighting a cigarette from a live end.

"How do you think *they* will take this kind of action?" He played his ace.

"In affairs of the heart the royal prerogative is simply a rubber stamp, and if I fall out of favor I can always live in France and on *my* money. In comfort, Tommy." She paused, dragged on her cigarette and broke into a spluttering cough. "If you want a scandal or threaten me with exposure," she added, "remember the courts will be on my side and I'll crush you. You'll finish your days in the provinces without comfort, an elderly homo running after young boys who won't be persuaded to eat black pud and drink cheap vino in filthy digs."

It was a bad dream. This simply couldn't be the plain, dull Duchess of Hampton who'd been on the shelf until he'd performed his rescue operation.

"I can live with your cynical self-interest, but I refuse to foot the bill for your appetites any longer," she continued.

He felt exposed and frightened, as he had as a child in the old, gray fieldstone council school he'd gone to. White-faced and trembling he came out of the bathroom and faced her.

"What do you want me to do?" he asked, forced to accept her terms of surrender.

"What do I want you to do?" she repeated, stubbing out her cigarette. "I want you to act like a man!"

She slipped off her white silk robe and he was confronted by a supple but muscular body, and for the first time in years he felt overcome by the mastery of her need and desire.

CHAPTER 9

"I'm intrigued," Nazem told Angelica. "In fact for the last day I've lived on the edge of a precipice, wondering what you've got in mind for me."

"*Who*, Your Royal Highness. You are a man who thrives on mystery, and I wish to prolong the sweet agony of speculation."

"Angelica, you're a treasure. Truly."

He looked at his watch and saw that it was close to midnight.

A short stroll along the Coronet, dinner at l'Oiseau and three hours of having his senses titillated at Angelica's by the two young French girls who had performed so ably the previous evening had drained Nazem's remarkable energy. He lifted a weary arm, placed his soft white beret over his damp forehead and left. He decided to walk for a while and his bodyguards followed at a distance, as did his car. Although he would have been glad to climb into bed, he was overcome by a strange restiveness whenever he found himself in the center of Mallacca. He lived with the omnipresent fear that he was in danger of missing something.

He stopped for a last drink at the American Bar before going back. But there was no one of interest in the bar except the usual girls looking for a late date. He avoided them. All they were good for was to service desperate married men on a two-day pass from their wives. An observer of human frailty, Nazem had in middle age become as interested in the actions of others as in active participation. After all, he had done everything that his fantasies had dictated, so he satisfied himself most of the time with the intrigues of others, calling this form of activity "investigations."

His attention was diverted by a tall, dark-haired girl picking up her key at the concierge's desk. Something familiar about her. Yes, the English model, very shy and not much of a talker. He had met her once before. He noticed Von Kuhl come in from the garage, just on her heels. He too picked up his key and joined the girl. They both waited for the elevator, rather self-consciously avoiding looks or words. From behind the cigar kiosk he watched them.

Nazem congratulated himself for not going directly home. Something definitely in the wind, and he wondered how he could best exploit the situation to glean the maximum satisfaction out of it.

He was just thinking of how best to get in touch with Madeleine when she walked in with Ricardo. She walked past the desk and Nazem called out after her. Ricardo, obviously embarrassed, waved to him and went up alone.

"Will you join me for a drink? I've some interesting things to tell you," Nazem said.

"On the condition that I buy you the drink."

"Agreed," he said, clapping his fat hands together.

She ordered a magnum of Dom and tried to hide in a corner, but there had been a loud whisper upon her entrance and Nazem enjoyed the speculation that hummed through the room. What were people thinking? They must have been mentally stripping the clothes from the two of them and wondering how they would look making love.

"To what I presume is your newly found happiness," Nazem said, raising his glass in a toast.

"Thank you, my friend," she answered quite freely. Nazem had listened to stories about her encounters before and had even provided the necessary refuge when she needed it. "The extraordinary thing is that I never felt any attraction to Ricardo. He's always been Carla's friend and I respected their relationship although I thought that it was dangerous of them to try to outsmart Giovanni who's always three moves ahead of everyone. But I suppose I've always wanted what Carla had. It's curious, because I love her. She's the best friend I ever had and what I've done is unforgivable. But sex controls my behavior," she added, winking.

"And so it should, *ma petite*. We define ourselves by the lengths we are prepared to go for it. Extremes . . . we'd be nothing without them."

"I've never thought it out clearly, but I suspect you're right."

Nazem was silent as the waiter filled their glasses again. And then he said casually, "I think you will have a perfect opportunity to be rid of Fritz."

She spilled her drink and he could see that she hadn't counted on this kind of revelation. Fritz's power and money had given her new status, and despite their frequent quarrels she wanted to keep him toeing the line. Good, respectable, gentlemanly Fritz. The suggestion was outrageous. It hurt her pride.

"What are you saying, Nazem?"

"I think he's found a playmate for himself. He walked in like a man in love."

"Who was he with?"

"No one, or rather he pretended to be indifferent, but I could see a certain tension in his attitude when he avoided the girl."

"Which girl? One of Angelica's?"

"Hardly." He was enjoying the little drama. "An English girl."

"Don't you know her name?" Madeleine demanded shrilly.

"She's the model. Decidely not my type, so I never could remember her name. She's been on a great many magazine covers."

"Maureen Polley!" Madeleine spat the name out as though an insect had flown into her mouth.

"Yes, that's it."

"What made you think that the two of them were together? I mean a man can talk to a woman . . ."

"It was the way he ignored her. Fritz is such a brilliant businessman and such a feeble actor. Germans all wear their hearts on their sleeves. It's a national trait."

"Maureen lives with that actor . . . Brian—whatever his name is."

"I took the liberty of making some inquiries. Teal is at the Casino and will probably be out all night. And I assume you and Fritz did not arrange to rendezvous at a particular time or place."

"He knows that when I have a script meeting—and he believes I have them—I can be hours, so we never make any arrangements." Nazem called for a new glass and Madeleine, eyes blazing, drank two glasses of champagne. "I don't believe he'd try anything."

"Shall we bait a trap?" he asked. "Or are you frightened to find out?"

"Frightened? Don't be a fool. I just hope you're wrong for Fritz's sake. Because it will be very expensive for him if he's caught. Angelica's is one thing, but I won't be made a fool of right in the Carlton."

"I thought only men practiced the double-standard," Nazem said slyly.

She sat there, chewing over the crumb of Nazem's suggestion. "Well . . . ?"

"All right."

They decided against telephoning the rooms and then hanging up, for this would give the two warning if they were together.

Madeleine still refused to accept Nazem's slender suspicion as proven fact. Of course Fritz wandered from time to time. It was natural. But there had never been anyone who had posed a serious threat to her. She sat impatiently waiting for Nazem who was discussing the situation with the concierge.

"I've told the concierge that we're playing a practical joke on a friend," he explained when he returned to her. "There's a vacant room next to Maureen's with a communicating door that is locked." He brandished the key "Usually they are locked on both sides but sometimes guests leave them open, carelessly. In any case, this is a skeleton key—the old traditions still live in the Carlton."

"That means that there will be a fairly large opening for the key."

"I wonder who ever said that actresses are just beautiful and stupid."

"Someone who never met me."

Tiptoeing down the hallway, Madeleine was overcome by a sense of the ridiculous. If anyone should see them, the inevitable conclusion would be that she and Nazem were having an affair. The idea had never before occurred to her and for an instant— No! No! Although she had to admit there was an insane, morbid fascination about the prospect. Like all who knew Nazem, she too had been entertained and had entertained others with his heroically perverted adventures. There were tales of nuns in the Congo, children in Cairo, bestiality in Kuwait. Infamy upon infamy, none of which Nazem ever denied. He never admitted to anything either. Apparently he had done everything and been satisfied by nothing, and now the pair of them, this mountain of a man whose enormity contradicted sexual activity of any kind, and she, Madeleine Maté, had decided to spy together. Was he the incarnation of Satan or just a rolypoly busybody who had run out of ways to amuse and satisfy himself?

When they were inside the room, Nazem pressed his ear to the connecting door, nodded his head to indicate that there were voices, then kneeled to look through the keyhole.

Fritz was there with Maureen, but Nazem was disappointed to find them both dressed.

He whispered hoarsely, "You look now."

She leaned forward and trembled with the nervous thrill of spying. She wasn't certain that she wanted to catch Fritz. It would make Nazem privy to her personal failure, and like most self-centered women she wanted to share only her triumphs.

She saw the girl first, sitting rather primly on the settee. Fritz was sitting in an armchair smoking a cigar. The scene suggested a comfortable married couple reviewing their day. Fritz had a curious ease and informality about him that she hadn't ever noticed before. In company he usually sat silently, half-listening to the conversation and contributing nothing except the money to pay. Here—difficult to explain—he wasn't the business technician attempting to put together the sophisticated aspects of a financial pyramid, but he exhibited the same kind of expert calm as when he knew all the answers. It was difficult to follow the conversation because there was so little of it. She could see Maureen either nodding or shaking her head negatively.

Nazem touched her bare shoulder. His hand was sticky with perspiration.

"Perhaps I was wrong," he said. "But they are together."

"They can't be talking business, that's certain, and yet Fritz's attitude is so odd."

"Quiet . . . I've just heard . . . Listen . . ."

"What? She pressed herself hard against the wall and skinned her knee.

She heard Fritz's voice quite clearly now.

"You'll tell him when he returns," he said.

"I don't know if I can go through with it. I'm scared. He gets so violent."

"If he does, you simply call my room and I'll be up in two

minutes. Now there's nothing to worry about. He's a bully and frightened of his shadow. I know the type."

"Fritz, are you sure? Really sure that it isn't an amusement."

"Don't be silly, dearest. I'll settle with Madeleine. She's only interested in the money anyway. And she's become an expense that I can no longer justify emotionally."

Madeleine shrank back. The idea of Fritz discussing her the way he would an unprofitable investment tore at the ego she had built up over the years. She was alarmed by her reaction. He had hurt her and she had supposed that she was invulnerable. Somehow, all of her petty slights, her indiscretions, her casual affairs, her insulting behavior toward Fritz and his family had been summed up on a bill which she wasn't prepared to pay.

"I want to go," she told Nazem.

"Look now. They're kissing."

"I don't want to see!"

"He's slipped his hand under her dress and she isn't pushing him off."

"So he's having an affair. Why shouldn't he? After all, I do exactly as I want. Please, let's go. I don't feel well."

As she walked shakily back to the elevator, Nazem took her hand affectionately.

"Madeleine, remember that when you want to get your way, there's no one who can prevent you. Can anyone refuse to yield? You have only to make the effort."

The elevator stopped on her floor and she nodded sadly, kissed Nazem's cheek and started in the direction of her room. He followed for a few steps. As her door closed, behind it he heard the explosive sound of a woman crying hysterically. She wasn't the love goddess that the papers and magazines had created over the decade, just a woman whose husband had had enough and was now discarding her.

Paul Martell's chief minister of state, Councilor Baguette, waited impatiently for the Count to come down to the cabinet room. Forty years of Mallaccan politics had made him cautious and noncommittal to a degree that enraged all the young hotheads who pleaded with Paul to replace him. Paul, however, was not adverse to playing politics and although he assured the members of the council that it was just "a question of time before I find a replacement," he had no intention of removing the venerable old manipulator.

Few statesmen have ever survived forty years, and Baguette, who had the ability to dance quickly on moving sands, had seen strong men executed, juntas destroyed, revolutions evaporate overnight and coups d'état fail without a shot being fired. Dictators and democrats had crumbled before his eyes, and sly old fox that he was, he managed to remain on friendly terms with the successors of successors. He had never been guilty of misplaced loyalty, for he had none to give. Mallacca was a pebble in the sea, and offered no strategic advantage to either conqueror or aggressor. It did, however, have its own unique banking laws, most of which had been initiated by Baguette, so he counted among his personal friends finance ministers of all the important countries, for his goodwill was necessary in preventing runs on weak currency, and for quick illegal conversions.

No, he was much too valuable to dismiss, Paul thought, making his way down the grand staircase, an exquisite wrought-iron mesh of delicate webs created by Florentine craftsmen for his great-grandfather. On the ground floor off the Hall of Echoes, were his study, the principal salons, the dining room, and the cabinet room. Paul wore a dark blue, double-breasted business suit with a thin white tie whenever he had an official meeting, in order to create the impression of a busy man of affairs who regularly rushed from one board meeting to another.

At sixty-five, Baguette had a head full of silver-gray hair, the carriage of a Prussian officer, and the rather low-keyed manner of the professional diplomat, having grown up in the school in which catastrophe is discussed as calmly as one's breakfast egg.

Baguette rose to greet Paul. He was a respecter of tradition and his loyalties were rooted in the time-worn pomp and circumstance that royalty visits upon civil servants.

"*Bonjour,* Monsieur le Comte," he said.

"*Bonjour,* Monsieur Baguette. Please be seated. Would you care for some coffee?"

"I have had my breakfast, thank you." He opened a battered cowhide briefcase and removed a thick file, which he placed in front of Paul on the long, highly polished rosewood table. "Some interesting facts have come to light since I began my investigation," he said dryly, and Paul knew that a bomb was about to explode.

He picked up the file which was headed: ARCHIMEDES PENDELOS, HOLDINGS IN MALLACCA.

"You need not concern yourself with the entire contents. I've made a summary on page one."

"Let's see. Bank holdings—fifty-two million pounds. Why is he holding so much sterling?"

"I refused permission to convert as a favor to the governor of the Bank of England."

"Arki must've been hit pretty hard during devaluation."

"So was the governor," Baguette replied.

"Swiss francs, Deutschmarks, dollars . . . this represents how much?"

"I believe sixty million dollars. There is also a gold bullion cache whose value we have not been able to ascertain since it is being held in bank vaults controlled by one of his companies. The real estate value of his properties is the alarming figure. Apparently, whenever he wanted a piece of land, you simply allowed him to purchase it."

"He paid the required tax," Paul said defensively.

"That is true, but the fact is he now owns half the island. On a large plot of land, he could dictate the terms, because he had greater liquidity than anyone else in Mallacca and did not have to remit money."

"It's all ocean-front property according to the map. It looks like a plan of some kind."

"Yes, it does, doesn't it?" Baguette said, a worried look tightening the skin on his face.

"His single most valuable asset is still the Casino. My God!" Paul stormed. "Value—a hundred million dollars! How is that possible?"

"If anything it's undervalued. Based on his net profit which is, of course, tax-free, he picks up nine to twelve million a year. I've used a multiple of ten years. That, my dear Count, is what it's worth. And the lease spells out his rights. They are incontestable."

"Incontestable," Paul repeated, feeling giddy with fear.

"That was your principal reason for having me investigate, was it not, Monsieur le Comte?"

"It was." Paul played with his platinum fountain pen and squiggled on the summary sheet. He had the sick taste of defeat and panic in his throat. "We get our rent from the Casino and that is all?"

"Yes. If Pendelos defaults, we can seize his property and assets in the amount of the default and assess him a suitable fine."

"Is there no way out?"

"Short of a national emergency, none, I'm afraid."

"Is there no morality clause that could be used?"

Baguette threw back his head and laughed—it sounded like a lion's roar to Paul—and tears clouded his small brown eyes. He wiped his glasses with his handkerchief and blew his nose regaining his equanimity.

"Forgive me, Count, but just about everything—short of dope and gold smuggling—is legal in Mallacca. Prostitutes are taxed and encouraged to come, so what constitutes a breach of public morality? Only one thing apart from smuggling, and that is not paying your bills, and Pendelos can pay his handsomely. If you tried to get him on morals, why you'd have to have everyone arrested, even the chief of security—your cabinet."

Paul glanced at the map of Mallacca. Arki's property was shown in green.

"It looks to me as though he is planning a resort area and there is no competition. This constitutes a monopoly, does it not, Baguette?"

"We have no laws against cartels, monopolies or trusts as they do in other countries. And if you're thinking of raising taxes to force him out, may I respectfully submit that you will have to tax all landowners and not just Pendelos, and this will cause great hardship and limit investment, which is precisely what you don't want to do."

"There must be a way out of this," Paul said to himself.

"We do have a housing shortage and Pendelos owns the choice land. If you were to buy back the land and put up blocks of apartments, parks and public facilities, you could force him to sell in the name of national interest. But you would still have to pay him for his land, and find funds to invest in housing developments."

"The man's invulnerable."

"So it would appear," Baguette replied, smiling slyly.

"I don't think there's anything amusing about this situation."

"Forgive me, but I had a small thought."

"Yes, well, out with it," Paul said fiercely. "We're about to go bankrupt!"

"Your grandfather was in more straited circumstances but we managed to survive disaster."

"How is it possible? Other countries go to the World Bank for loans. We are not members, and even if they were prepared to loan us money how do we pay them back? What do we use as collateral? I refuse to sell parcels of what little land remains to foreigners."

"I admire your spirit, Count. The little thought I had will require great courage on your part if it is to succeed." Paul waited impatiently for him to continue. "A national emergency."

"What the devil is a national emergency? Is it the fact that I can't pay my tailor or the builders for repairs made to the palace?"

"The National Emergency Act of 1932, which I had the privilege of drafting, is an enabling act. It gives the government, that is, you, with the consent of the cabinet, extraordinary powers."

"None of this means anything to me."

"It gives you the right to suspend the constitution."

"And how do I go about that without being assassinated by my own people?"

"You nationalize the banks and property. All Mallaccan citizens have the right to be landowners for a small licensing fee. This prevents the people from rebelling. It's simply a bit more money and they can keep their property. But it prevents foreigners from keeping theirs."

"Baguette, that's a positively brilliant scheme."

The councilor bowed his head graciously and accepted his due with modesty.

"Furthermore, you can keep your foreign investors by adding a rider that a Mallaccan citizen must be in control of the majority of voting shares in any company. Archimedes will come immediately to you. He will protest, he will threaten, blackmail you if he can, but there is nothing he can do. You, Monsieur le Comte, will gain control of all assets as controlling director. That is the only way he can save anything. There is, needless to say, sufficient precedent for nationalization—Egypt, England, France, not to mention the Bolshevik Revolution. You at least are prepared to offer partnership to foreign nationals. Other governments have simply sequestered property. All this in the name of national emergency."

Paul embraced the elderly councilor who, as a respecter of royalty and nobility, shrank back in shock. He had found a way to save his Count and country and he was grateful to be of service—and in the process to nail the coffins of the young hawks who had closed ranks to force him out of his position as senior councilor. He was neither senile nor tame in a fight.

"One favor, Monsieur le Comte?"

"Name it, Baguette."

"According to law I must be retired at the end of my sixty-fifth year. It would make me more confident if you suspended this law as well, and enabled me to act as first councilor until my death or resignation. I have felt currents, dangerous to our little country, blowing through the cabinet room over the past year."

"I shall do it by royal decree. When do you think these announcements should be made?"

"You will have the world's news services covering the gala. That might be a good time. A press conference at the palace afterward."

"You seem worried, Arki," Toni said, as they walked along the silver-sanded beach. She liked being barefoot and alone with him for a change. They were always surrounded by guests, visitors, financial advisers and the curious. She waited patiently for his reply and when he continued walking by himself she stopped by the water's edge.

"Aren't you listening?" she asked.

He turned, gestured with his right hand like an explorer greeting uncharted land.

"I think we'll build here. I'd like to be on the beach."

He pointed to a small natural bay shouldered by beach pines. It seemed an ideal spot—shaded, with a natural inlet for a boat landing. Olive and lemon trees grew in abundance on the small hillside which could be shaped into a garden.

"What do you think, Toni?"

She came toward him, kicking the water as she moved, her face puckered with displeasure.

"Didn't you hear me?" she asked.

"No. I'm sorry . . . had you asked me something?"

"Yes, you seem so preoccupied and worried. Can't you tell me?"

"It's a business problem, that's all."

Under the palm tree the wind had cooled the air, and she sat down on the sand. No, this wasn't working out the way she had planned it.

"Aren't you feeling well?" he asked solicitously.

"Fine, just fine. Look, let's get one thing clear from the beginning."

"Has someone been talking to you about Marta or was it Marta herself?"

"God, you've got a guilty conscience about her, haven't you?"

"Not in the least. She's been well provided for and my conscience is quite clear."

"Look, your past is your business." Her top was sticky with sand and she slipped it off, then stood up to pull off her trousers. She wore a white bikini underneath. "I haven't been a little den mother myself. What bothers me is the fact that you won't confide in me."

He sat down next to her, rubbed his hand along her sunburned thigh, then pulled her face close to his and kissed her affectionately on the cheek.

"I'm touched. Really touched by your concern. It never occurred to me that the woman I loved would want to share everything in my life. The mechanics of making money are tedious even to those who employ them with some skill, so I won't go into the details with you." He paused and she held his hand tightly entwined with hers. "There've been rumors here in Mallacca about some change in the law that can affect me."

"Does it involve Paul?" He nodded. "I thought he was simply a figurehead."

"He is because he's chosen that role. The fact remains that the power resides with him."

"Well, what could he possibly do to you?" she asked. The idea seemed preposterous. Paul was always running after young girls, or dressing up in his ceremonial uniform to greet a visiting dignitary or organizing a gala for some charity. He seemed as harmless as a fly, a dabbler in delightful things, astute at small talk. "I can't believe that he could hurt you."

"My darling girl, Paul is broke. When I took over control of the Casino, it was failing. I put it on its feet, agreed to pay Paul more than I should have, but still it's not enough for him. He sees the money that can be made and now he feels cheated. But the fact is, he has no talent for business. He's indolent and without imagination and merely a pawn in his chief councilor's hands. But if Paul is as desperate for money as I've heard, he could take over the Casino or for that matter all of my assets. There are no tax or banking treaties that I could fall back on in a court of international law because Mallacca has no conventions with the rest of the world."

"Is this all just rumor or do you have proof?"

"Two members of the cabinet who have worked with me in the past and have tried to get rid of Baguette informed me that an extraordinary cabinet meeting will be held today. I control half the property of Mallacca, apart from the Casino. I have enormous sums on deposit in the banks here, as well as gold bullion. Do you know what liquidity is?"

"Actual cash and assets."

"Exactly. Well, they can damage my liquidity and this would make for an awkward situation since I have holdings in other countries that depend on these assets."

"It sounds so complicated."

"It is!" His eyes shone with demonic fierceness and she shrank back. "I'm sorry I told you. My instincts told me to keep my own counsel."

"I wanted to know. There's got to be a way out of this."

She laid his head on her lap. And gently, she embraced him with a sense of great maternal tenderness that she had never before realized was the better part of her character.

CHAPTER 10

Susan had lain awake all night. Her mind was cluttered with problems that surrounded her like ever-growing ant hills. She and Paul now slept in single beds. When she'd been pregnant with the twins and continually waking Paul by her restlessness, she had decided out of consideration for him to sleep by herself. The arrangement had suited him perfectly and when after the twins' birth, she had wanted to go back to the double bed, he had insisted on continuing to sleep alone. And although most men found Paul weak and cloying, he exerted a remarkable degree of authority over her.

She ignored with success the fact that he was a spendthrift, lazy, vain, and unscrupulous with his friends, and concentrated on his still-boyish charm. She even ignored the fact that he seldom played with the children, and was often impatient with them. She had not been strong enough to correct his character deficiencies—perhaps no one was—but she continued to live on the edge of hope. Angelica's lesson had certainly not fixed matters yet, but maybe it would lead them back to a double bed.

She crept out of her bed and stood by the window. The first rays of the sun came through the curtain and illumined the foot of his bed. In two hours, the palace would be bustling with servants, and she would once more be caught up in the unvarying routine of her life. Fifteen minutes with her daughters, then breakfast with Paul. He would read his paper, she would look at her typed schedule. She would make her visits to orphanages, hospitals, charity bazaars, old-age homes. If there were official visitors, she'd attend to luncheon or a cocktail reception. Sometimes there would be a state dinner, purely ceremonial, since no one needed Mallacca's political goodwill or economic assistance. In any case, Mallacca had none to give. She was a hair on the world's body.

Susan knew that if matters didn't take a real turn for the better, Paul would leave her. He'd find himself a young heiress and milk her until she had nothing more to give. The daughters of Mexican and South American millionaires had contributed to Paul's upkeep before Susan. Girls whose fathers had enormous wealth in copper, oil and cattle had in the hopes of gaining a title been outsmarted by the wily count. When the girl found herself in trouble, Angelica arranged an abortion. Paul had managed to avoid marriage and Susan now realized that she had been picked because of her position, name, connections and family wealth. Dollars were in, and South American currencies out. Marrying a Villanueve or a Lamata was simply not the same as having John Pratt Belmont as a father-in-law.

What Paul had failed to consider was that her father had the ferocious temper of his shanty Irish mother, the thrift of a Scotsman, and the self-importance that old money provided. John Belmont had decided to limit his communication with them to the card he sent to the twins on their birthday. That card was always accompanied by a notification that the girls had been given another thousand shares of the Belmont conglomerate which was held in trust by himself, so that neither Paul or Susan could get their hands on it.

Susan studied the slack mouth, the long oval face, the tousled steel-gray hair of her sleeping husband and decided that she would make another effort to save her marriage. She had a warm bath and perfumed herself with Eau de Mallacca. She brushed her long red hair back and slipped on a thin, short silk night-dress.

As she lifted the sheet off Paul he stirred irritably, opened one eye partially, then closed it and turned on his side. Angelica had given her a small vial of the powder that Susan had used on her tongue with the young man. She now knew that it was a cocaine derivative mixed with an aphrodisiac. She slipped into bed with Paul and was surprised when he made room for her. Her hand moved down his thigh and she felt for his limp member. She gently massaged it with her hand and rubbed some of the powder on the tip. Slowly, it grew in her hand and then she moved down the bed, got on her knees and put it in her mouth. She tensed the muscles of her lips to create a viselike grip and moved her head up and down.

Paul opened his eyes and watched her with some surprise.

"You've found a new way to say good morning," he said.

She stopped for a moment.

"I want to make you happy."

"I think you've got yourself an old lover."

"There's never been anybody but you."

"What have you put on me? My cock's tingling."

He smiled with lordly pleasure as he watched her move her head. For years he had tried to persuade her that there was more than one way to make love to a man, but she had resisted. She had insisted that she'd choke to death. Now, he thought, it was all too late. He was too deeply involved with Angelica and had become used to a variety of sexual fare. Whenever the mood took him, Angelica would arrange something different to arouse him. The day before, he had watched the new English girl reach her orgasm with a dog that Angelica had trained. He recalled Joan's expression when the dog mounted her. He'd never seen anything so frenzied in his life.

Susan attempted to move her head away, but he seized her neck and forced her farther down, until she began to gag. He let her up slowly at his convenience, then forced her head down again. Her eyes were wide with fear.

"Again! Again!" he commanded.

As she moved down, he came.

When the hot semen entered her mouth, Susan thought she would vomit. Paul held her tightly, using her mouth as if it were a vagina, and forced her up and down. She didn't know what to do and swallowed it. When he sighed and leaned back on the pillow, she jumped off the bed and rushed into the bathroom. She was dizzy and horrified and she hung over the sink feeling the nausea tear through her body. Paul came in, looked calmly at her and picked up his toothbrush and began to brush his teeth. Speaking with a mouth full of toothpaste he said:

"You've got a white moustache. It suits you, Susan." He rinsed his mouth and she turned away as he put an arm around her. "With a little more practice, you might be as good as a professional." He did not see the tears in her eyes.

Around the long table, Paul surveyed the faces of his cabinet. In addition to Baguette, there were six members, all elected by popular vote the previous year, and for the first time in Mallacca's history the average age of the members was under forty. For some time, there had been considerable pressure to initiate constitutional reforms. These changes, as Paul and Baguette foresaw, would infringe on the powers Paul had been granted and would alter the political character of Mallacca. There would be a constitutional monarchy and Paul would become a mere figurehead, living on a fixed allowance. His authority would be ceremonial. Despite his ineptitude in dealing with political and economic matters, he was determined to hold to his guaranteed rights. Cabinets had come and gone, duly elected, and suffered through their four-year terms, fomenting revolutionary ideas which ended in pure frustration, for Paul refused to "alter my country's history for the worse," as he put it.

The sight of Baguette by his side fluttering thick folders of papers offered the council members something to wonder about. What new bit of chicanery had Paul prepared for them?

"May I know the reason for this extraordinary meeting?" asked Meuse, the contentious young deputy who was also the island's principal builder.

"You will be told shortly after my opening remarks," Paul replied curtly.

"The cabinet has no meeting scheduled until the autumn," proclaimed Gervais, the real estate dealer who had inherited one of Mallacca's great fortunes and whose political aspirations were limited by Paul's refusal to accept change.

"There've been rumors," said Justin, "about Pendelo's position on the island." He owned the largest department store on Rue d'Anton and he had found in Arki a business associate who had brought new prosperity to Mallacca.

These three occasionally got support from the other three members when the latter found their well-buttered bread in danger. But more often than not, Coutard, the meat packer, and Verrier, the perfumer, with the stolid backing of Mardi, the hotelier, joined together with Paul and rubber-stamped his proposals. All six members were, however, in some degree involved in Arki's ventures, and they valued his allegiance and courted him outrageously. Perhaps Justin had put it best when he said: "Archimedes' favors are golden," thus summarizing the others' esteem for the patronage of the Turk.

As Paul had always enjoyed good relations with Pendelos, it now came as a shock to the members to learn that the financier had territorial designs on Mallacca and had openly cheated Paul and Mallacca out of the profitable Casino. Meuse shook his head violently.

"It comes as a surprise to me, Count, to hear you accuse Pendelos of such deceit. Several years ago when your company ran the Casino there was a deficit of three million dollars. We have a guaranteed million a year since Pendelos took it over."

Gervais, red-faced and with the uncontrollable temper of an important man in a small place, interrupted, shouting:

"Half the land was under the sea! Without Arki's investments our very best property wouldn't exist. How do you think we've been able to pay for dredging and filling in the beach property? Good heavens, Count, what you're proposing is not only dishonest but could lead to disaster."

"Withdraw," shouted Baguette, alarmed by the accusation of dishonesty aptly thrown at Paul. "Withdraw," he repeated.

"I will modify my statement," shouted Gervais. "What you propose is financial ruin, and I refuse to be a party to it. What will a Mallaccan contract be worth in the world after this? Or the word of a citizen of the country? It will be synonymous with deceit and hypocrisy."

"Don't dramatize," Paul said coolly. "We face a national emergency."

"The Enabling Act was intended for use when Mallacca faced war!" Meuse stormed.

"Where does it say so?" Baguette asked dryly.

"It implies a state of war," Justin replied hotly.

"It is a question of interpretation," Baguette said. "It calls for giving the Count special powers in time of national emergency. Nothing more nor less."

"The state of the treasury demands that I use these powers," Paul added.

"Why not ask Pendelos for a loan?" Gervais suggested and the other members nodded agreement.

"I'm certain he will give you one," Coutard said, wavering.

"We need assets, not further debts," Baguette said with finality.

"Shall we put it to a vote?" Paul said, anxious to terminate further discussion. "All those in favor say Aye." Paul and Baguette raised their hands and said "Aye," followed a moment later by Mardi and then Verrier. Coutard abstained, and the three others vociferously voted against the proposal. "Carried four to three with one abstention," Paul concluded.

As the three in opposition angrily rose, muttering threats of press conferences, censures, and public repudiation of the Count, Baguette cautioned them.

"You gentlemen are aware that these proceedings are confidential. If the press or the public learns of this before the Count's press statement, you will all be liable to arrest and forfeiture of your properties. Is that clearly understood?"

Outside on the steps of the palace, Justin took out his handkerchief and mopped his brow, and Breitner and Pinot, standing on the deck of the *Archimedes*, picked up the prearranged signal with their powerful binoculars. The two men looked dispirited and went silently below to Arki's offices to inform him that he had been defeated by Paul.

Never having suffered defeat before, the two men were left without a constructive idea between them. Too many financial coups, too many raids on the market had deprived them of the necessary posture and reconstruction that must take place after one has suffered a blitz. Forlorn and desperate, they confronted their mentor, attired in his usual white pants, bare feet and blue polo shirt. They were shocked by his calm manner that said everything and nothing. What did the man have up his sleeve? Surely his friends at the Turkish Ministry of War and Security hadn't put warships at his disposal. The idea was patently absurd. Pinot whispered to Breitner while Arki nonchalantly discussed money markets with Zurich. If there was a way out, Arki would find it.

The Grand Ballroom was arranged with one hundred tables that would each seat twelve guests. Workmen hurried to and fro like black ants. Ernesto, in his major domo tails, ordered maids, waiters, silver-polishers, and stewards to greater heights of activity. Susan watched him with a rapt expression of admiration. She had already had meetings with the musicians who were busily practicing in the orchestra pit, discussions with the chef de cuisine and his staff on the menu, and with the program director who would also serve as master of ceremonies. Marta Torres, dancing her "Swan Lake" solo, was to be last, an English group known as the Flying Caterpillars would be first, and Robert St. Louis, the new French piano virtuoso, would be second. She fluttered her hands and Ernesto stopped for a moment.

"Yes, Your Highness?"

"I have to leave now for an appointment, Ernesto, and I wonder if there is anything more you'd like me to do before I go?"

Her question was, she knew, superfluous, for Ernesto, like a Napoleonic general who had already won the decisive battle, had everything under perfect control.

"No, Your Highness," he said gallantly, "I believe I can now manage. Thank you for your gracious attention." He bowed low from the waist, clapped his hands for the others to stop and acknowledge the Countess's departure.

Susan checked her dress and makeup in the private downstairs dressing room and nervously left by the south gate to avoid running into any ministers or Paul. Her Lamborghini waited for her in front of the garage as she had ordered and she drove out the rear entrance.

Angelica wore a mauve flower-patterned dress well above the knees and carried a lavender parasol. From a distance she looked like a schoolgirl on her way to a garden party. It was only when you were close to her that you realized that she was one of those ageless women. Perhaps it was the clothes she wore or the omnipresent suntan which, despite the beauty experts, did not crinkle her skin. Probably, Susan thought, her youth came from her attitude toward life, an easy acceptance, a refusal to worry, and an absolute contempt for everyday problems that drove other women mad. She had turned her back on the trivial worries and managed to see things in proportion. Once, she had told Susan: "The only thing you should concern yourself with is a fatal illness and if it's fatal, well, why worry about it?" A childhood disfigured by poverty had not soured her disposition, nor had later financial comfort made her complacent. She had found the perfect balance between business and pleasure. She neither defended her manner of making money nor suffered from the occupational hypocrisy of her profession.

"Ah, Susan, I thought you might have been held up at the palace."

"There were a great many things to do, but Ernesto has proved to be a treasure."

"I was lucky to find him for you. When he came to me he was desperate for a position, for he was without references. You know that he had difficulty in Sicily with the Mafia and was given a choice: either to leave the island or *omertà*."

"I didn't know that," Susan said, somewhat alarmed by her major domo's history.

"He was asked to help a Capo blackmail his employer and he refused. So you've nothing to worry about." She laughed girlishly, with her head thrown back. "I'm sure there are few secrets he doesn't know about."

"You seem to know a good deal about him. Does he keep in touch?"

"Well, he still has many connections in Sicily and on the mainland, and from time to time he recommends a girl to me."

As she neared the junction of the Moyen Corniche, Susan slowed the car.

"Just continue on the Corniche, Susan. It isn't far."

"Who are we going to meet and why?"

"Well, I've given the matter a great deal of thought—your problems and Paul's naturally—and the fact is if you had *un bel ami* these financial details that plague you both from time to time could be resolved."

Susan gripped the steering wheel so tightly that her hands were almost numb.

"Oh God, Angelica, it's such a terrible mess. To think that it would all come to this! We were the golden couple when we got married, and now I've got to offer myself for sale like a common streetwalker."

"If you think of yourself as one, you become one. It's all a state of mind. In my time I've been forced to do things that would make any woman shudder. In the Spanish village where I was born . . . well, there was nothing to do but to try to make enough money to feed a starving family, when my father got lost at sea. I was ten when I began—ten, Susan. Every night I waited patiently by the docks for the boats to return and then the men came in hordes. Sometimes fifteen or twenty in one night. I never had the courage to turn anyone away for fear that they would not come back. When steamers docked from South America carrying rubber from the plantations in the Amazon and there were peons impressed on board along with crews of murderers, I went aboard. The captain gave me a dollar a man or sometimes a flat fee for everyone, everyone! And when my mother came to buy food nobody asked questions. None of them wanted to know—the butcher, the grocer, the vegetable man, the dairy—just pay the money. My mother didn't ask either. Every morning when she got up she found money in the family Bible. So it was holy money, given by God to his deserving servant. She preferred to believe that, but Susan, my body knew the truth."

There was a long silence broken only by Susan's thanks for the cigarette proffered by Angelica.

"What would he . . . expect?" Susan asked in a trembling voice. This, she knew, was not going to be like the lesson in love Angelica had provided her with.

"I'm not certain. His tastes run to . . . well, how shall I put it . . . young things . . . innocents or those with the appearance of it. In any case, let's not worry about it. This is simply a discussion."

In spite of her nerves, Susan laughed at this description.

"God, it sounds like a stockbrokers' conference."

"There, you're feeling better already. It's the anticipation that frightens you. Happily, I was cured of these fears when I was a girl. What can one possibly fear, human or beast?" she said darkly. "One's own imagination conjures up more demons than actually confront us."

Angelica had no way of knowing whether her plan would succeed. But if it did work, she could lay claim incontestably to Paul's affections. It was, after all, Susan who had presented him with the enormous financial burden that drained his resources. If she could get Susan off Paul's hands the Count would openly take her as his mistress. Somehow the prospect of being Paul's mistress was more exciting, more tantalizing, than the respectable status of a mere wife.

The electric gates of Nazem's villa slid open silently. Four men came out from the gatehouse, all armed; they looked abashed when they saw the two women, and waved them on.

"Are we meeting him here? At Nazem's?" Susan asked in astonishment.

"Yes, I thought this would be the best place."

"Can we count on Nazem's discretion?" Susan asked, suddenly sickened by the intrigue.

"I'm absolutely sure we can."

Susan stopped at the edge of the portico where Nazem, wearing a baggy white linen suit, smiled and waved to them. He removed his sunglasses and approached the car, held the door for Susan and helped her out.

"My dear, how kind of you to come," he said. His glasses were part of his face, like his unkempt black beard. Susan had never seen his eyes before. They were like black marbles and she was taken aback by the luminous physical beauty of them.

"I thought we might have tea in the garden," he said, taking her hand and leading her to a soft chair at a table already laid. "It's a glorious day, isn't it?"

"Yes, just glorious." She could not help staring and he noticed it.

"Is something wrong?"

"No, it's just that I've never seen you without glasses."

"My eyes are sensitive to light."

"Oh, you do tell fairy stories, Your Highness," Angelica put in. "He wears his glasses so that people won't see what he's really thinking."

"Angelica is so clever that when we think we have taken an intelligent line with her, we can be certain that she's thought of it five minutes before and discarded it as too clumsy and unimaginative."

Susan sat down and Angelica excused herself to go into the villa to examine Nazem's new wing which was in the process of construction. She had acted as friend, agent, and bully during Nazem's absence, and the workmen shrank back when they observed her coming, busying themselves with hammers and saws.

"She's my construction boss as well," Nazem said, amused. "The workmen take turns missing work when I'm here, so when they see Angelica they stop the monkey business."

"We're fortunate to have such a friend, aren't we?" Susan said, watching Angelica disappear around the back of the house. Susan noticed that there were only two cups and she watched with some consternation as Nazem poured tea. Finally she had to ask. "Aren't we expecting someone else for tea?"

"Who?" Nazem appeared puzzled. "I suspect Angelica will allow us our tête-à-tête without interruption."

"I'm not quite clear . . ." Susan felt herself grow hot and uncomfortable as a suspicion too horrible to contemplate formed in her mind. She sat silently looking at her white shoes.

"No other guest is expected," Nazem said with finality. He handed Susan her cup.

"I don't understand." She played with the teaspoon nervously.

"I thought Angelica had made it quite clear. I've always been one of your silent but nonetheless ardent admirers. Isn't the feeling mutual?"

Susan dropped her cup. The tea stained her white dress. Surely this was a monstrous mistake. Small, pudgy white hands were touching her dress. A wet cloth was being rubbed over the stain.

"Leave it!" Susan said sharply. She took a cigarette from a box but her hand was too unsteady to light it.

Nazem's small lighter flickered under it. He was speaking rapidly to her. "I must face the reality of my personal appearance, so I try to live my life as imaginatively as possible. The only thing I put my faith in is the pleasure principle. It is the only thing we can fall back upon. Susan, have you been listening?"

"I can't believe what I've been hearing."

"Why not? Doesn't it seem to be an obvious solution to your problems?"

"What do you know about my problems?"

"Well, Paul's financial state has been a subject of public discussion for more than a year. How do you think he lives? If it weren't for Angelica, you probably wouldn't have electricity."

"Angelica! What has she got to do with Paul?"

"Nothing—never mind," he said, quickly trying to cover, but at the same time glad that he had reached her. Damn Angelica; he'd assumed she had broken the ground.

Susan sat back. It was all happening too fast. Her mind couldn't contain it, and her eyes closed. The taste of bile welled up in her throat, and she fought against the sick feeling. When she opened her eyes she saw him looking at her legs.

She felt herself pulled to her feet and assisted across the lawn. The living room was cool and Nazem drew the curtains to shut out the white light of the afternoon sun. In the darkness, she lay on the soft silk couch and gained a momentary composure. She mustn't think. She listened to Nazem's strained wheezing. His cigarette smoke curled into a moving fog, then rose to the ceiling.

"You were telling me a little while ago about Paul and Angelica."

"What can I tell you that you don't already know." To hell with Angelica, he was thinking.

Susan was rigid with shock. And yet, at the same time, she was not completely lost. Something began to jell in her. It was obvious to her that Angelica and Paul had not only used her but also despised her. She was determined now to destroy them. The thought gave her strength.

"May I have a drink?"

"Yes, of course. Scotch?" She nodded. He fixed them both long highballs. "Fortunately my religious vows no longer deprive me of this civilized pleasure. We were a nation of drug addicts because religion forbade alcohol. Drugs are all well and good, as long as they don't use you."

She sipped her drink, then her head cleared and she felt a totally unexpected surge of strength. It was truly extraordinary—rather as though a marvelous wine had entered her. So Paul had betrayed her and it was public gossip. Worse, it had appeared that she had condoned the liaison. The sense of humiliation was sharp, but she was not destroyed by it. She must play the game, be lured into Angelica's trap in order to defeat Paul and Angelica. Because she was going to defeat them. The thought was wonderfully sweet to her, and so was her marvelous new confidence.

"I'd very much like to hear what you have in mind," she said, and Nazem spiritedly moved closer and sat on the edge of the couch. She rubbed his back with her stockinged feet and he responded by gently massaging her legs.

"I am prepared to take care of you, my dear Susan, so that you are not troubled by such tedious problems as the absence of money." The thought of corrupting Susan, making her a partner to his diversions excited him. What a conquest! The Countess of Mallacca! Any price would be cheap. Yes, she'd be the perfect permanent friend. This conquest would provide new fuel for his fantasies.

"What do you expect of me?" she asked, and almost laughed as she listened to the sound of innocence in her voice.

Nazem's fat cheeks spread in a smile. "Much as I respect the nature of a platonic relationship, I have never been privileged to enjoy one. Heaven knows I've tried, but something in my character prevents me."

"Your appetite," she said simply.

"I suppose my body is the perfect mirror of it." He waited for her to disagree, to say something euphemistic about glandular irregularities, but she held back. "It should bother me, but it doesn't. I have had what I wanted and I still want."

"Novelties? I thought you'd had just about everything you could dream of."

"With one notable exception. A respectable woman to share my special interests. We could come to some arrangement."

"That's a nice way of putting it."

"Circumstances dictate manner. The last thing I would do is offend you, Susan. We've known each other some considerable time and the truth is the first time I met you in Hollywood there was something about you that crept into my heart." He closed his eyes and saw the scene again. "You were not the Countess of Mallacca, and I was a king and I daresay I was more attractive than I now am. Try to remember—was I of interest to you?"

"God, that seems another life ago. Did I live through it?"

"Of course you did. With remarkable success. You threw it away for Paul. It all seemed plausible at the time. The American princess marrying the European count and going to live in his fairy-tale kingdom. In practice it has not been so wise."

"I loved Paul." And for a moment she felt a pang as she thought of those early days—and nights.

"He was bankrupt and attractive, you were an heiress and beautiful. A perfect example of America's coming of age. Innocence corrupted by experience. Americans as individuals seem to live out their country's history. Nowhere else is that true."

"So that brings us, or rather me, to the Villa Nazema in 1970 to reconstruct the crime." She jingled the ice cubes in her glass, then rose to make another drink.

"To a woman in your position that's all that's left, new experiences."

"Where is your construction boss?" Susan asked suddenly.

"My car took her back to town some time ago. She's served her purpose," Nazem added brusquely.

"I was under the impression that you two were good friends."

"The variety of my appetites forces me to enter into relationships that seem personal but are nothing more nor less than business. Angelica gets well paid."

He switched on a lamp and opened the top drawer of the massive partner's desk that stood facing the window. He removed a thick brown envelope and brought it to her. It settled on her lap and she made no attempt to open it. Her interest was stirred, but she concealed it.

"Paul and friends. On eight millimeter."

"He allowed you to take them?"

"He wanted to use my villa. The owner has certain privileges, does he not?"

"So he didn't know that you were photographing him?"

"He wouldn't have acted quite so—so candid if he knew. People do ham up these things."

"Do you want me to see them?"

"Whenever you like. I'm in no great hurry. They do reveal a side of Paul that I hadn't realized existed. I never credited him with so much imagination. Perhaps it was Angelica who inspired him. Do have them. I have another set."

She got up, stuffed the envelope into her handbag and lit another cigarette. The room was curiously comfortable and much to her surprise she had discovered that she was at ease with Nazem. Almost in spite of his grotesqueness, his Gothic exaggeration, she had discovered he was remarkably fascinating and sly. A thought crossed her mind, then she discarded it, for it was so sinister as to belong to the realm of nightmare.

Susan finished her cigarette and took her departure. As she put the weight of the bulky envelope in her handbag she thought of her children, and for an instant she weakened. But the knowledge that she would be acting in their best interest asserted itself.

On the drive back to the palace she toyed with several ideas. Then as she saw the *Archimedes* moving into a harbor berth, she knew exactly what she would do.

CHAPTER II

Supervising the arrangements for the pre-gala cocktail party aboard the *Archimedes,* Toni felt again the pleasures of being queen of the international scene.

The table was simple and exquisite. Deep gold dishes bedded in chopped ice filled with Iranian caviar; tubs of Dom, fresh salmon and Strasbourg pâté de foie gras with truffles. The floral decorations were unobtrusively dainty.

Arki had made dozens of phone calls when they came back from the mainland and now his spirits were high. He was silently pleased, as if he'd discovered a way out of his dilemma.

Deborah, still in her bikini, was drinking champagne, casually watching the arrangements.

"Look at me getting quietly pissed," she said to Toni. "Who would have thought Arki would put such stars in your eyes."

Toni put some caviar on a bit of toast, handed it to her sister and watched her wolf it down. It brought to mind the old days when Deborah used to sneak into the study and sample the liquor. There was that same expression, puckered lips, narrowed eyes, hand over her mouth, so that their mother wouldn't smell her breath and Deborah could pretend that she'd been sleep-walking.

"You've got to promise me something, Deborah."

"Where do I sign?"

"I'm serious." Toni took the champagne glass from her and sipped the remainder. "I want us to be together like we have been. I don't want my marrying Arki to make a difference. I love you both and as far as I'm concerned that's what it's all about—sharing and being with the people who really matter. But you've got to change your attitude toward Arki."

The amused, playful smile left Deborah's face and she stared out at the sea. The cool breeze as the day closed began to chill her. Was it too much sun and champagne or the turn the conversation had taken?

"Let's not forget certain hard realities," Toni continued. "If Nick earns a hundred thousand a year, it's a great deal of money. He's a director of a couple of companies in London, and they sort of keep you going. But he's really just a glorified p.r.o. Arki can change all that."

"What are you suggesting? That we aren't showing due respect to our master?" Deborah replied, white with anger.

"I don't think you have any conception of the kind of power Arki has," Toni said. "We're not talking about someone who was clever enough to make a few million dollars, but someone whose wealth is in the hundreds of millions. It intimidates everyone, even you. That's why you're behaving stupidly."

The thought of her marriage inspiring jealousy in her sister and personal friends alarmed her. She had planned to create a court in which all the good, talented, loyal people she knew would find a home—no matter what the rest of the world thought.

"Arki said that he'd be glad to have Nick work for him," Toni lied.

"Doing what? Holding his coat, or answering the telephones?"

"That isn't fair, and you know it," Toni said, her cheeks flushed. "There are probably any number of places in Arki's companies that would be perfect for Nick."

"I'm sure there are. But what would happen if you and Arki had some trouble? Where would that put us? Social contact is one thing, but business is very different. Or let's say Nick accepted a proposal that Arki made—how would it work out for you, if Arki wasn't happy with the way Nick was doing the job?"

"Why don't you let me worry about that? And darling, nothing's more obvious than an old affair. So let's be big girls about it," Toni said.

They were both relieved to have the conversation interrupted by the arrival of Pedro, their hairdresser, who had flown in from Paris. Following him down the gangway was Jacques de Charlus accompanied by two women carrying an enormous box.

"Jacques, dear, I didn't know you'd be the first to arrive," Toni said with some chagrin. She had ordered her gown from Balenciaga and it would be awkward to appear before Jacques wearing his competitor's creation. He embraced her, then hugged Deborah.

"My two favorite sisters. *Allons, mesdemoiselles,*" he said, waving the two women forward.

"I'm a little confused," Toni said, staring at the two French girls balancing the box between them. "Are they . . . ?"

"Seamstresses, just in case my work is less than perfect. A surprise, Toni."

"Did I order . . . ? God, I am a scatterbrain. Pedro, you can do Deborah first."

As Deborah prepared to go below, Toni took her arm and whispered; "You'll see. Everything will work out. I'm counting on you. Now more than ever."

The sisters held tightly to each other and Jacques, amused by the scene, clapped.

"I thought the wedding was to be next week," he said.

"Oh, you rat, you Frenchman, you know everything. I'll bet Arki proposed to you first," Toni said.

"Let's go, Toni, we haven't much time."

"I wish somebody would explain what's going on," she said as Jacques took her arm and led the way to her room.

"I've brought a petticoat, just in case you didn't have one," Jacques said when they were in her bedroom. "Come on, get those pants off," he ordered. "Jacques knows every square inch of those thighs, so stop pretending you're embarrassed."

"You've got a dress for me!" Toni said.

"That, my dear Toni, is like describing the queen's crown as a hat."

"I refuse to pay. I'll take it on appro."

"It's paid for. If you don't like it, I could always melt it down," he said with a flourish, lifting up her hair and unbuttoning her top.

There was a moment of silence when he opened the box, then Toni broke into hysterical squeals of delight, which brought Arki rushing into her room. Toni threw on a robe over her bra and panties and reached up to kiss him.

"Arki, you're blowing my mind."

"I was too smug to ask if you like it," Jacques said.

The two seamstresses held it up for Arki's inspection and he moved his head in approval.

"I don't blame you for not asking, Jacques," Arki said, fingering the lustrous white satin, which, with its interwoven diamonds forming a heart with its cleft at the bodice, resembled an intricate fan made of butterfly wings.

Arki embraced Toni and said:

"You'll look like a queen."

"Whether I do or not, I'll feel like one."

"We'll be a while before we fit," Jacques said. "I want to close this seam and then see that it's properly ironed."

Arki led Toni out of her cabin, instructed a steward to assist Jacques and bring in a bottle of champagne for the two women. In his cabin, he sat her down on his sofa and slipped his hand under her robe.

"I can't resist you when I catch sight of your bare skin."

"In that case I'll walk around naked all the time," she said, unbuttoning his shirt.

Keeping Arki off balance was a difficult game, for he had experienced the tricks and techniques of beautiful women for years and could usually anticipate them. But Toni was different. He never knew what to expect from her, and her effect on him was as potent as an aphrodisiac.

"Switch off your squawk box," she said, indicating the radio telephone on his desk.

"Just press the button down."

She found it, then sat on his desk and opened her legs carelessly, so that the gesture seemed uncontrived.

"Have you ever had it in your office?"

"It's dangerous to ask a man questions about his past."

"How many hundreds have you had right across the desk?"

He smiled slyly, enjoying the game. "I wonder if I ought to tell you?"

"Tell me, Arki. Tell me, please."

"Well, if you come over here and sit on my lap, I might be persuaded to remember."

She got up quickly and sat across his knees. Then she played with the snap on his beltless trousers.

"Now I want to hear and don't leave out a single detail."

He cleared his voice, rubbed the small of her back and lifted her hair to kiss the nape of her white neck.

"No monkey business until I get the whole story."

"Well, my darling, believe it or not, this is the first time . . . in my office."

"Oooh, you're such a fink. Here I've got myself all excited to hear the juicy details about you and Marta and five thousand starlets. It's not fair to let me down."

She stood up and paced, her forehead wrinkled, then she slowly removed her robe and began to dance in front of him. He clapped his approval. The white line of her breasts was in sharp contrast to the bronze color the sun had left. As she danced she opened her mouth and rotated her tongue over her lips. She edged one of her breasts out of the bra, and drew close to him, within touching distance. She anticipated his move and darted quickly back. She swirled around the room on bare feet, graceful as a breeze, and he felt his tension mounting. She danced by the side of the desk, picked up the Dictaphone mike and slipped it into her panties.

"The next time you talk, you'll think of me."

"Impossible child . . . I love you."

She inched off her white panties and continued to play with the microphone.

"Did Marta give you this kind of treatment?"

"No, she didn't," he said with some hesitation.

"What was it like? I want to know," she insisted.

"Like stepping into your slippers after a bath."

"Oh, that's awful. My poor Arki, having to make love to a slipper." She came near him and he took her arm and forced her back down on the sofa.

"You're driving me quietly mad."

She tickled his ear with her tongue.

"What is it like with me? Putting on your pajamas?"

"No," he laughed. "It's like the sensation I get when I have the flu. Dizzy and lightheaded."

She moved up and down on his legs with her eyes tightly closed. He moved his head close to her exposed breast, kissing it as she sighed.

"Oh, darling, I feel alive." She covered her mouth with her hand to stop herself from screaming, then in a sudden spasm of anguished passion she let it fall and yelped, "I felt you coming inside me. It was so hot and good. Maybe we'll have a baby."

"A baby?" he asked in alarm. "Why?"

"I ran out of pills the other day, and I don't care."

She couldn't stop the tears that trickled down her cheeks and he wiped them with the corner of his shirt.

"Toni, why are you crying?"

"Can't I cry when my man makes me happy?"

The unanswerable question was the child side of her that he adored and would preserve as long as she allowed him to restrain her growth in the hothouse of his imagination.

Oddly enough, Carla thought that Ricardo seemed younger than ever. Somehow the infidelity with Madeleine had removed the careworn lines from his face, and she noticed that he smiled more often now, rather shyly. The endless conflict of their affair had made him appear deeper and more serious than he actually was. Over. It was over, she told herself, mouthing the ugly final word with distaste. Although she knew that it was a fact that she'd have to learn to live with, she still could not believe it, for it was almost like accepting the death of a real person. A true love affair becomes something outside the people who create it, a tangible force that exists like air and is not any the less real because it is invisible.

Walking along the quay with Ricardo just before the party, Carla felt he might have been a casual acquaintance she hadn't seen for years.

"Is Giovanni going to join us?" he asked in a lifeless voice.

"He's making some calls to California. He'll be along a bit later."

Just be civil to Ricardo, she told herself, nothing else is necessary. People stared at them, but they were accustomed to it. She had wanted to walk because she didn't want to chance creasing her skin-tight black silk gown in a car.

She dreaded the party, but to stay away would be an admission to the tongues that had begun to wag that something was wrong. Her appearance with Ricardo would allay any suspicion. They were still a few hundred yards from the boat when Ricardo stopped at a flower-seller's. He picked up a long white rose and gave the vendor some loose change. He handed the flower to Carla who looked at it with a mixture of puzzlement and resentment, thinking that this was a feeble attempt to make peace. But by the same token, he had admitted nothing about Madeleine. The subject had been avoided and, as surely as an eyewitness account, this had provided her with proof. Yet Madeleine had not crowed on the beach that afternoon, nor had she been unpleasant to Fritz. Perhaps she'd imagined it all, and Ricardo had nothing to hide.

"What's the rose for?" she asked.

"Do I have to have a reason to give you a flower? Just a whim —and it goes nicely with your gown." He held onto her arm and felt her pull away slowly. "Is something the matter?"

"You tell me, Ricardo. I don't know. There's something . . . I'm afraid to put it into words. It's like when a scene doesn't play. There's no need to discuss it. We know it instinctively."

He stopped several feet from the edge of the dock where guests shouted effusive greetings to Toni and Arki and their assembled entourage. He led her to a corner stall which blocked them from the view of those aboard. His dinner jacket felt rather too tight and sweat dripped from his top lip. He wiped it with a handkerchief.

"Tears and perspiration," she said. "They both taste the same, don't they?" She waved the rose back and forth like a fan, and his eyes, heavy and limpid, followed like a baby teased with a rattle. On the stall were fresh clams, oysters still with bracken and weed attached, and long, curling langoustines. The man in the stall worked carefully with his knife-opener and made no attempt to entice them.

"I don't know if this is the time . . ." He faltered and stared at the display of fish.

"I'll let you decide when. I did my dying last night and dead people have all the patience and time that the living don't."

"Oh, Carla, don't be melodramatic."

"I was stating a fact. I suppose I should have known that Madeleine would one day betray me. What else are friends for? You give someone a pint of blood. They recover and run off with your husband. It's the way of the world and just because we're in films doesn't make us any different. We're not exactly trend-setters at infidelity. In a way I'm not sorry. We had a bit of magic that people dream about, you and I, Ricardo. The jewels are still there but in the vault, and paste is safer in public, isn't it?"

"I can't explain what happened," he said, looking gravely at her.

"You don't have to. I've got enough imagination for both of us. I'm not even bitter toward Madeleine. It's curious. But the point is, she must have been desperately unhappy to do this to me. So I have the advantage. I can survive my own disasters, she can't. That's one of the differences between the two of us."

"I can't go on without you," he said with conviction, and his need touched her.

"It *was* the other way around. But you'll be all right. It's only sentiment now."

It was a painful scene she played and she thought, If I don't get to the party soon I'm going to cry and I'll never be able to stop. "Let's have some champagne, drink to the future and to old loves."

His mouth twitched and she smiled, for it reminded her of one of his famous scenes—he had been caught by an irate husband with his young wife and the audiences had roared with laughter. Ricardo's terror had seemed so real that it was funny.

"Carla, I couldn't help myself. I tried to resist, to fight, but . . ."

"The Vichy collaborators used the same explanation after the war. But, darling, no one's going to shave your head or put you in prison for yielding."

She started for the boat, forced a smile to her face and Ricardo,

like a Judas goat gone senile, stumbled after her. Arki came toward them, bowed from the waist and embraced them both.

"With you, I avoid *les baisers français*," he said, kissing Carla
full on the mouth. "Fortunately, what one does in public one
doesn't have to explain in private."

"I thought you were in love," Carla said.

"Can't I love Carla as well?" he asked Toni.

"I'll allow that," she said, and the two women embraced. "Oh,
dear, when I look at your figure, I know what I'm missing. You
bring it right home."

"There are certain small differences between a Volkswagen and
a Ferrari," Carla said, throwing the white rose over the side.

"Not everyone is raised on pasta, Carla dear."

"Hasn't Giovanni come?" Arki asked, swiftly mediating the
scene.

"Business calls. Do you think everyone is as well organized
as you? He still counts his pennies and telephones collect."

Carla watched Ricardo stand at the far corner of the deck
looking out at the harbor. At parties he was always so awkward
and circumspect, never enjoying himself unless Carla stood by
his side amusing everyone and making the few words he spoke
seem like wit worthy of Oscar Wilde. He was also drinking too
much, she observed. Perhaps Madeleine would be good for him.
He'd become worldly or drown in the effort.

Although Madeleine had arrived with Fritz, she'd made no
move toward Ricardo or Carla. Odd behavior for someone on
the first leg of an affair. The conspiracy struck her as badly
played. They'd learn after enough scenes together. She made her
way toward Fritz who had turned to talk with Nick. She noticed
his eyes roving through the milling guests, searching for someone.

"Am I what you're looking for?" she asked.

"I'm always looking for you."

"When you can't find Madeleine."

"I can never find Madeleine, and I save myself a lot of money
by my failure."

She was rather surprised by the edge Fritz displayed. Out of character. Or perhaps they'd come to a decision and would see lawyers sooner than expected. He looked over her head while Nick kissed her hand and babbled something about new English representation for Von Kuhl Industries.

"Where *is* Madeleine?" Nick asked Fritz.

"We arrived together, which astonishes *me* more than anyone. No doubt she's found herself a seaman who wouldn't know the difference between salmon roe and caviar, and she'll instruct him."

"Fritz, is something wrong?" Carla whispered.

"Actually, Carla, things could not possibly be better—for me."

"In love?"

"Yes, and for the first time. Extraordinary sensation. I feel like a schoolboy who's suddenly discovered the difference between the sexes, and I'm so happy I don't trust myself. In fact I prefer not to trust myself and to discard the logic of three hundred years of German philosophy. I'm not drunk or drugged, but my newly born sense of freedom makes it appear so. Is Giovanni to honor us with his company this evening? I see Ricardo has been unleashed."

"An owner has certain responsibilities to a pet."

"I'm happy to see that romantic agonies no longer plague Italy either. Perhaps we wouldn't have joined forces to lose a war if we'd known all along."

"Fritz, you're positively sparkling tonight. I thought you were a walking financial report."

"French propaganda. What they don't understand, they ridicule. And Madeleine is, of course, true to this national character trait."

Madeleine had appeared just as Fritz finished speaking, but she remained silent, and avoided looking at anyone. She had decided to hold her peace and play the complacent wife. Perhaps if she overlooked Fritz's little flirtation he would return to the fold and they might begin anew. She realized that she genuinely wanted him. Ricardo had been like the others, an adolescent's thrill, and she wondered why she'd even bothered. There hadn't been anything remarkable in his lovemaking, simply passion squeezed out like a pimple. If only she could talk it out with Fritz.

Ricardo, a bit uncertain on his feet, came toward Madeleine.

"We've really made a mess of things, haven't we?" he said.

Just behind them a group of Italian musicians began to play "The Girl From Ipanema." They strolled through the milling guests.

"Somehow it was necessary," she said blandly.

"For whom?" He sipped the last of his champagne and before he had a chance to put the glass down, a waiter took it and handed him another.

"Well, when you put it that way . . . for me, if it will make you happy."

"Nothing can make me happy. Except"—he paused and stared out at the blinking lights on the buoys—"if I believed that you cared about me. But the truth is that you thought Carla had something you wanted, and now you discover that she's welcome to her little amusement."

"Giovanni knew about you. He told me," she said.

"And so for a part in his rubbishy film, you were asked to do him a favor?"

"No, he didn't ask anything of the kind. That was my own idea. I know it won't seem plausible to you, but I thought Carla would be happier without you."

"Oh, dear Madeleine, you're not suddenly going to tell me you're an altruist."

She turned away, rubbed her eyes with a handkerchief. Everything was falling apart, friendships broken, ungrateful lovers, lost husbands. She looked past Ricardo at Fritz brimming with good humor, tanned, handsome, a thoughtful, passionate lover, and knew that she'd have to work hard.

"We, or should I say I, get what I deserve. And what I deserve is nothing . . . nothing, Ricardo."

Standing in the center of the crowd and conscious of the fact that everyone's eyes were on her, Toni thought of herself as Cleopatra reborn. There were some striking differences—she was prettier and Arki's fortune made her considerably richer. Cleopatra's barge was a wooden tub by comparison with the *Archimedes*. And Toni was queen not of a country but of world society. She had broken out of provincial America to become royal lady of the world's capitals.

She looked forward to the Paris fashion shows, shopping in Rome, the Cannes Film Festival, Christmas in St. Moritz (Sun Valley was out), dancing in London discothèques. Her one visit to Annabel's Club had brought a barrage of small-minded criticism from American papers. But now she could dance all night with anyone she chose to.

Her appearance at charity events had always been noted by the columnists, but now there would be front-page stories. She enjoyed her celebrity—she always had—but there had always been those who sniped at her and found her behavior scandalous. In politics the yokels' views had to be taken into consideration, the President had cautioned her. Her preference for French designers had disturbed those patriotic Americans who thought that she should wear matching sweaters and skirts of a discreet length.

She listened as the people near her spoke in undertones, commenting on her dress and the Black Star Diamond on her finger. She pretended not to notice the diamond and smiled in a slightly withdrawn manner when people remarked on it. Simply part of the furnishings. By accepting everything without excitement, she emphasized the fact that she was a queen by divine right. Even Gavin, who'd begun to assert himself, stood spellbound by her side, watching the level of champagne in her glass the way a doctor might an intravenous bottle.

Pedro had designed a new hair style for her. A black wig set in a crown of curls with a tiara of pearls. The black hair was a perfect complement to the diamond-spangled dress.

When Nazem arrived with his entourage of bodyguards and a new girl, Toni turned to her gallery of admirers and asked:

"How does he manage to make love with that stomach? Mirrors, I guess."

Gavin and Mulholland as well as Arki bellowed their appreciation of her wit. A throng of newsmen and photographers, noisily complaining about Arki's refusal to admit them to the boat, made an attempt to crash on the heels of Nazem. Toni moved to the rail and waved at them and they responded with a resounding cheer. Telephoto lenses were directed at her like cannon and she smiled graciously, then with a serene gesture of command motioned them away. Good press relations were born out of instinct.

Nazem paid her the compliment of bowing and then hugged Arki.

"I am so happy that you have at last taken this step," he said.

"I wasn't certain that I'd have the courage."

Nazem turned to Toni.

"Don't let him follow my example. I had the courage seventeen times. And now look at me."

"Maybe I've got the enthusiasm of seventeen," Toni replied, studying the girl behind him. Nazem didn't bother to introduce her and she overheard a voice saying, "Joan Somebody or other. Probably one of Angelica's new girls."

"They're all new for a week," a woman said.

"And that goes for Toni as well," the man replied.

Toni stopped a waiter and motioned for Joan to take a glass of champagne.

"It's lovely to have friends," she told Joan, smiling at the couple who beat a retreat when they realized she had overheard them.

Once Toni had given Joan the royal stamp of approval, a group of people joined them.

"Nazem's new queen," Toni said.

"For the night," Joan replied.

"Well, that's good enough for me . . . and *everyone* else."

She could make a whore respectable if she chose to and no one dared disagree.

CHAPTER 12

Maureen listened fearlessly to the pounding on her door. She gave herself a last once-over in the mirror. Her canary-yellow satin dress with a high mandarin collar and matching shoes and bag looked very good indeed. She'd caught some sun and the tan highlighted her outfit. There was a hoarse shout in the corridor and she smiled at herself, and opened the door.

"Where the bleedin' hell've you been?" Brian shouted. He was still in beachwear and his polo shirt was rakishly knotted around his neck.

"I could ask the same question."

"Left you a note, didn't I?" For a moment he was disoriented. "And why'd you change the room?"

"Preferred my own, that's why."

He forced his way past her and shoved her into the room.

His nose was the color of a skinned tomato and he disconsolately examined it in the mirror.

"Listen, love, I don't like anyone to put me on."

"I'd get dressed if I were you. I had your dinner suit pressed, and your tie and shirt are out."

"Considerate of you," he said with a snarl.

"I think it was, even if you don't."

"Were you about to leave without me?" he asked incredulously.

"We've been invited to a cocktail party and *I* want to go. Want, Brian. And I'm used to going places on my own. I've had enough practice."

"Moving out the minute my back's turned," he said, dropping the cockney barrowboy's mannerism. "I don't know what's got into to you, Mo."

"I've had enough."

"Got a bloke, have you? Touch of the light romantics and a poke after tea."

"Don't talk to me like that," she said spiritedly, and he turned from his mirror reflection to stare at her with his mouth wide open.

"Close your mouth, Brian."

He put his hands around her throat and was about to squeeze.

"If you touch me you'll get your head broken."

"I can't believe you're talking to me this way, Mo."

"Good-bye, Brian. You better borrow some cash from a friend, because I'm not paying your bill this trip."

"What?" he asked dumbly as she walked quickly to the door. But she was gone without an answer.

He returned to his room, saw his clothes neatly laid out, and blotted out of his mind the scene with Maureen. He stripped, let the water run cold and stepped under. He recoiled from the shock of it, but forced himself back under. After a while it wasn't quite so painful.

Dressed in his black velvet dinner suit with a lace shirt and attached tie-scarf, he resembled nothing so much as an eighteenth-century court fop. But it didn't worry him; he drew the stares and the clucking of all the regulars in the Carlton lobby, so the performance was justified. He stopped at the concierge's desk and attempted to find out if Maureen had been seen with any man, but Fritz had already tipped the concierge so well that the man would have perjured himself at a murder trial.

As he strolled jauntily down the quay, Brian spied Ambrose-Smith stumbling down the gangway of the *Archimedes*. He went up to him, placed an arm around his shoulder and said:

"So this is where it's happening."

"You look positively gorgeous, Brian. Come on and have a drink. Maureen's here. She swallowed up half the men when she arrived. You two have a lover's quarrel?"

"Somefin' of the kind. But it'll be all right."

"I love her flat chest. It's so in. I'm getting a little fed up with all the tits squirming out of their—their—restrainers. She's got such good taste."

Led like a baby to the deck and capturing the attention of the fringe of the assembly, Brian said hello to Arki and Toni who treated him with a graciousness he never deserved but always received. Champagne was forced on him and he did little to protest, although he cautioned them about other parties.

"Expected all over the place," he lied. "Should've had a social secretary."

Brian wasn't certain if Toni actually remembered him, and in spite of his show of confidence he said awkwardly:

"We met the other night at the Casino. I was playing with your sister," he added.

"She did pretty well, I think."

"Won herself about fifteen hundred." He stared at Toni. For the first time in his life, he felt thoroughly dominated. Just the sort of woman he should have. Someone he could look up to and admire. He could certainly learn from her.

"I'm sure I've seen you somewhere else," Toni said.

"I've made some films. P'raps *Borstal*. That was my big one.

I played a boy in prison who was set upon by the warders. Then I died in solitary after they beat me."

"Yes, I saw it. You were marvelous. When are you going to have a new one out?"

"I'm in the process of picking a few projects. Does Archimedes like movies?"

"Arki? They put him to sleep, I'm afraid. But I'm a fan. In fact, I think he's got an interest in one of the film companies."

"Really?" Brian said with undisguised interest. "Do you know which one?"

"I think it's something with Giovanni Mosca."

"Ever done any acting yourself?"

"Me? I never got beyond the pledge of allegiance. I freeze just thinking about it. But Deborah was always interested in acting. In fact—"

"I still am," Deborah interrupted, and cast a gleaming eye on Brian who extended his hand. "You weren't trying to make off with my lucky charm, Toni."

"I've got my very own."

"And one's enough for any girl," Deborah said laughing. She handed Brian a caviar canapé from her plate.

"Sorry, I can't. Stains my teeth."

"We have to pay a price for everything, don't we," Toni said, moving off. Deborah was glad to have chased her, but she noticed with irritation that Brian's eyes followed Toni.

"I played Ophelia and let's see what else—? The Narrator in the Shelby Girls' School production of *Our Town*. And lots of other things."

"That's terrific. I'll bet you were great. You've got the voice for the theater." He looked at her full-face, then profile. "It's a cert that you'd photograph really super."

"Do you really think so?"

"No question about it. I'm surprised that Mosca or even Arki never suggested it to you."

"Arki?"

"Toni told me that he was in the film business."

"That is interesting. But there are so many things to learn. It'd take years."

"Nonsense," Brian said firmly. "Just a few tricks and a good lighting cameraman. If you were serious, I'd be willing to help all I could."

"You're a dream, Brian. An absolute dream."

Brian took the compliment in his stride, but he felt a distinct flutter in his stomach. He'd destroy Maureen if it was the last thing he did. The ingrate.

He looked over at Maureen, surrounded by a dozen men near the hors d'oeuvres table. She looked doe-eyed; she had on her famous incandescent smile as compliments flew like flak through the air. Could be any one of them, Brian thought. One thing he'd always admired about Maureen was her ability to keep confidences. Probably easy for her, she never opened her mouth, except to say yes or no. Tommy tugged him away from Deborah.

"Well, old cock, enjoying yourself?" he asked.

"Quite a bash, in't it? You're stayin' wiv 'em, Tommy?"

"Victoria won't stay at the Carlton. She says it's very unchic. I don't share her opinion. Brian, you look absolutely dishy."

"Like me clobber, do you? Touch it if you like."

"If we were alone, you wouldn't have to ask me."

"Still got your drum up in Putney?"

"Of course, where would I be without my haven."

"Wormwood Scrubs more than likely, or lingerin' round the mouth of the Piccadilly Station convenience, observin' new talent."

"We've a new gimmick," Ambrose-Smith admitted. In his cups he might say anything, and Brian looked for Victoria to clap a hand over his mouth. "We import au pairs, but they're boys. No law against keeping houseboys, is there, Brian?" A volley of fatuous laughter brought a sputtering cough with it.

"Good evening, Brian. I so hope Tommy's not making a nuisance of himself."

"Brian brings out my romantic side," Tommy said.

"I'm not amused by your behavior, Tommy," Victoria said, looking around fearfully and hoping that they were not being observed. "Do restrain yourself."

"Restraint's just what I need, Victoria. Get out the bonds," he said, thrusting his hands behind his back.

"Oh, God, I wish I knew what to do with him, Brian. When he drinks he's liable to do anything."

"Don't worry, I won't tell the truth," Tommy said captiously. "And in any case, Victoria, everyone knows about me unless this is a meeting of the flat earth society."

"They don't," she protested. "If I thought they did, I don't know what I'd do."

"Relax, Victoria," Brian said consolingly. "When he's had a few he kicks up his heels. It's a put-on, Tommy. Tell 'er it is."

"I will if you promise to be mine," he cackled.

"Please see that he doesn't have any more," she pleaded, firmly gripping Brian's shoulder. "As a favor to me. I can't control him when he's like this." She moved over to where John Mulholland was chatting with Nazem.

"Tommy's making a scene with Brian," she whispered to Mulholland. "Do see if you can get him away before he does something foolish. Please, John."

"That boy never knows when he's had enough," Mulholland said pompously. "I'll look in."

Finding herself alone with Nazem, Victoria felt flustered as he peered over at Tommy and smiled. In his country there was no need for discretion, and he secretly protested against the English need for good form. Another example of Western hypocrisy.

"Short of murder, why shouldn't everything be permissible between a man and woman?" Nazem asked with a slow grin.

"I didn't realize that you were a philosopher as well," Victoria replied.

"As well as what?"

"A former monarch."

"Oh, I thought you meant something else. And since you did, let me tell you that I stopped worrying about what other people thought when I was a boy."

"That is evident," she said with a slight sneer.

"I hope it is. I have one obligation in this life."

"It's remarkable that you've managed to simplify and isolate life's problems so systematically. I'm afraid that I haven't been able to work things out quite so easily."

He was enjoying needling her and watching her discomfort.

"Oh, it wasn't easy, not at all, I assure you. I had many people who disapproved and they made things difficult for me. But the purpose or should I say my obligation is to enjoy myself. Wilde once said that the only way to get rid of a temptation is to yield to it."

"He got what he deserved for his public performance."

"Perhaps all martyrs do. But, Victoria, do remember that what people do in public is less dangerous than what they do when they're forced to hide. Some people enjoy scandal; others don't survive it. I think you know what's important to you."

Deborah caught Toni's eye and they walked together to the pool area.

"I like Brian," Deborah said.

"So I noticed. But for God's sake don't make a fool of yourself."

"I have no intention of making a fool of myself," she answered with irritation. "The fact is, he's a very talented actor."

"I noticed that as well."

"Look, Toni, he had a really wonderful idea. To help me start an acting career."

"You haven't acted for years."

"But I was pretty good when I did."

"Yes, you were," Toni admitted. "You're really serious, aren't you?"

"It'd be a real chance for me. Something I've always wanted to do. I get so damned frustrated at times."

"Why don't you talk it over with Nick?"

"What's Nick got to say about anything?"

"Unfortunately true. But, Deborah, you don't need my permission."

"Arki's buying into a film company. He could help."

"Where'd you hear that?"

"Brian just told me."

Toni didn't have the heart to tell her that she'd made up the story on the spot, just to tease Brian. Deborah's mouth twitched nervously as she waited for Toni to reply. Be generous, Toni thought. She'd have a word with Giovanni and Arki about it all.

"Of course, Arki will help. If that's what you really want."

"I could become something," Deborah said hopefully.

Something more than my older sister, Toni reflected. She put an arm around Deborah's shoulder.

"You know I'd do anything to make you happy."

She watched her sister rush back to Brian. The two talked with animation. They were making plans. It was a pity that Deborah never understood that pursuit was the man's role. It was obvious now that Arki had run for his life.

Fritz, with Maureen in tow, like a man with a winning sweepstake ticket, approached her.

"My dear Toni. Congratulations."

"Thank you, Fritz."

"I don't know if you've met Maureen Polley."

"I've seen your face thousands of times," Toni said. "You're much prettier in the flesh."

"So are you," Maureen said. "Your dress is fantastic. I've never seen anything like it."

"Jacques designed it."

"I thought he did. It's incredible."

"You shall have the same one," Fritz said.

Maureen laughed and slipped her hand into Fritz's.

"It's incredible, absolutely incredible."

"Falling in love," Fritz said.

"Making love," Toni said with authority.

The three laughed and Maureen nestled her head on Fritz's shoulder.

"Madeleine's looking at us," Toni said.

"She can look all she likes," Fritz replied indifferently.

"What would you do, if you were in her position?" Maureen asked innocently.

"Murder you, darling. Murder you."

Marta Torres arrived at the palace in Paul Martell's official limousine. She was met by Ernesto and two maids who were to help her dress for her performance. Susan came down the staircase to greet her, and the two women, friends of long standing, embraced. There was a great deal to discuss. Susan led her to the ballroom and Marta tested the wooden stage that had been constructed. She found it to be up to professional standards and she relaxed. Often there was danger of slipping or jamming her toes if the floor was uneven.

Large draperies cut the ballroom in half. Behind the stage was a guest room and bathroom that had been put at Marta's disposal.

"Why didn't you get in touch with me when you arrived?" Susan asked.

"I didn't want to see anyone for a few days."

"I understand," Susan replied. She had tasted defeat, experienced humiliation and had passed from shock to constructive disillusionment. Perhaps the two of them could help each other.

Ernesto brought them some champagne and Susan raised her glass.

"To the end of innocence," she proposed, and Marta gave her an oddly surprised look.

"Is that just for my benefit?"

"For both of us," Susan said forcefully.

"Men think they're so clever, don't they? Perhaps we don't want to see everything and so allow them more freedom than they deserve," Marta said.

182 THE PLEASURE PRINCIPLE

"Everyone's been laughing behind my back for years," Susan said, "but they won't anymore."

"No one laughed at you—"

"My incredible stupidity. I never thought I was so naive."

"It wasn't stupidity. You simply trusted Paul as I did Arki. Any woman would've done the same."

Susan gave a rueful sigh.

"You weren't brought up in a tradition of intrigue and deceit, Susan. It hurts when you have to play by someone else's rules. Either you continue to play with them, give up the game, or play for blood. Which I intend to do." Marta's eyes flashed.

Susan sat quietly for a few moments, her chin resting in her hand. Her lime-green gown brought out her beautiful sadness perfectly, and yet her eyes had a fierce light in them.

"I can't quite get over it. Of all people, the most unlikely— Angelica. My friend."

"She worked on Paul for a long time," Marta replied.

"Did everyone know about it?"

"We all thought it was simply a flirtation on Paul's part."

"She's his mistress and all along she's been plotting against me."

"What else does a retired prostitute swimming in money have to do?"

"She even tried to matchmake, to get me off with Nazem!"

A mutual desire for revenge had made the bonds of friendship even stronger.

"Arki used me, paid well for the privilege, and I mistook cash for passion. But he chose Antonia Millhouse," Marta said bitterly.

"I know how to get back at Paul," Susan said. "But it means helping Arki. God, Marta, I don't know what to do."

"Will you be happier when you've got your revenge?"

"You bet I will. I want to make that worm crawl. It's the only way I can survive. I've got to get back at him. I never took any nonsense from the studio heads in Hollywood, so why should I let Paul trample me?"

The same thought had already occurred to Marta.

"Toni's the chink in Arki's armor," Marta said. "And I know exactly what I've got to do."

"You know I'll do anything I can to help."

"I was counting on you to help, Susan. What you can do is make sure that the future Mrs. Pendelos has a ringside table. She might add to the show with a surprise act."

CHAPTER 13

At night the fairy-tale kingdom of Mallacca came to life. The Martell Fountain spewing a hundred feet of water was splayed with various light combinations. Respighi's *The Fountains* came over a pair of speakers; in case the palace guests overlooked the fountain, they would certainly overhear it. Swathed in gold light, the palace appeared larger than it actually was. The formal gardens were also alight, and one could see a junior Fontaine- bleau grove. Liveried attendants in the green and gold colors of the nation formed a phalanx on the portico to usher in arriving guests. Paul, like all successful promoters, put on a show of strength when he was really broke. The attendants had been hired for the night from the Spanish Village. Most of them were fishermen and they smelled it. Still they looked impressive. The whole place had, for some incredible reason, the look of Hollywood in the thirties.

Paul, followed by Ernesto, inspected the facilities. In his study, reserved for intimates, he examined the cognac and brandy set out. Armagnac had been replaced by a one-star turpentine supplied by an obscure French vineyard, but the Armagnac bottles were real. On Havanas there was no cheating; since Mallacca and Cuba were friends and the price for big shipments of cigars was not throttled by duties, they were still dirt cheap. Paul looked like a real monarch—apart from the Croix de Mallacca, which he wore around his neck with a red ribbon, he had enough decorations to impress any career sergeant. He had the posture of a prince and the manner of a gigolo and was in his finely cut official uniform— gold jacket and dark green trousers—to distinguish him from the lackeys who were dressed the other way around.

Satisfied with the arrangements, he went into the library—a massive domed affair with about fifteen thousand volumes—which he used only for card parties, or to keep importunate favor-seekers waiting, hoping they would be so intimidated that they would forget what they had come for.

An early arrival waited there. It was Angelica. A peina held up the fall of her raven hair and she wore a chartreuse heart-bodiced gown. She was sipping Pastis and soda.

"We match," Angelica said, raising her glass. "I think I prefer you in informal clothes. You look too important this way and I ask myself how can I keep such a man happy?" The flattery worked—it usually did—and Paul broke into a smile to show his agreement. He kissed Angelica on the top of the shoulder and lightly touched her breast.

"If only we could have our own, very personal party," she said.

"We will, don't worry, darling. When I've announced our new financial reorganization I'll be my own man. At the moment I still need Susan's goodwill."

"She doesn't know what you intend doing?" Angelica asked in alarm.

"Naturally she does. As the Countess, she has access to all privy council papers and aide-memoirs. Usually she doesn't bother with them. But since Arki is a friend, she took an interest. I had to explain what took place. It would've been bad form if she had to ask one of the councilors."

"Oh, Paul, I don't think you did the right thing. She might go to Arki."

"Don't be silly. She's got too much at stake. Don't forget that she needs money also."

"I thought you were letting me attend to that."

"Well, did you?"

"This afternoon I brought her to Villa Nazema. I wanted to phone you afterward but I thought it might be too tricky—if anyone picked up the phone by mistake or listened in at the exchange."

"Quite sensible of you, Angelica." He sat down in a wing chair and lit a cigarette and then with a rueful smile turned back to Angelica. "What begins as an ideal, ends in irony. Susan and Nazem. I suppose it's possible. He can make up in invention what she lacks in enthusiasm." The configuration—Nazem and Susan— might have been amusing if it weren't quite so obscene. "I wonder if she'll really accept him."

"You seem concerned. Does it worry you?"

"Simply vanity on my part, Angelica. What you take thoughtlessly you give up with reluctance, oddly enough. Usually people think they want to preserve what they've fought for. In practice it's the other way around. Susan is my wife, just as the palace is my home. It's always difficult to forfeit someone else's position when it has been useful."

Angelica pursed her lips, but then smiled. She had to control her tension. To show weakness at this stage of the proceedings was to court defeat. Paul was weak. He preferred to talk, to theorize about events, rather than participate. It was a recurring failure in men who had inherited great wealth or position. The strong woman was as necessary to them as a cane to a gout-ridden aristocrat. If she revealed weakness or uncertainty, he'd bolt from the stable like an unbroken stallion. Dominated, he'd yield, just as he'd made Susan yield. Those who wield authority, she knew, required it even more than those who accepted it.

"I have no fears about our success," Angelica said with a show of confidence.

He beckoned to her but she refused to come. She remained fixed by the bookcase sipping her Pastis. He got up, came toward her and kissed her fingers, and she looked disdainfully at him. She was trained in men's weaknesses. He embraced her and she gently pushed him off. It was less a rebuff than the continuation of a lecture, and he waited for her.

"Paul, don't panic. Not now. Do you understand?"

Before he could reply, they were both startled by the silent appearance of Susan.

"At least we both give him the same advice," Susan said with cool amusement. "He's like a table with a wobbly leg. Remove the book and it shakes. Now perhaps we can talk—the triangle is complete and this kind of meeting is always stimulating before a party," she added.

"So now it's in the open," Angelica said. There was a quaver to her voice which gave the lie to her calm, self-assured manner. Paul averted his eyes and poured himself a large whiskey.

"Susan, darling, I don't see why we can't remain friends. I still care about you," Angelica said.

"So do I!" Paul added, at last finding an opening.

"The affection of some people is the highest form of insult," Susan said in a perfectly calm tone.

"What do you intend doing?" Paul asked.

"I don't think you're entitled to an explanation. Do you, Angelica?"

"He is still your husband. And he occupies a position here of great importance."

"He is my husband in name only and as far as importance is concerned, his own incompetence has made a mockery of his position. He's squandered tax revenues for years, watched his own people live in poverty without lifting a finger to help. He's also gone through my personal money with even less concern. It's altogether fitting that he fall back on you and allow you to support him. A whorehouse is now the national treasury. And a prince its pimp. But I think you might have given at least a thought to our children, Paul," she said, with contempt.

"What you're saying is a dirty lie," Paul said, beside himself with anger.

"Paul and I have known each other since we were children and we've been lovers for years."

"Well, I hope it will continue. You deserve each other," Susan said. "But perhaps now we might go to the party?"

A fleet of limousines stood waiting at the quay beside the *Archimedes*. The proud Mercedes 600 edged ahead of its rival, a silver-cloud Rolls which was boxed in next to a white Bentley convertible. Beside the stately mastodons were a medley of Ferraris, Aston Martins, Masseratis, Lamberghinis and Jensens. A million dollars worth of ornate machinery stood ready to transport the owners the six city blocks to the palace.

The steward in consort with Ernesto would make a twenty percent profit on the food ordered for the occasion, thirty percent on the alcohol, and no one in Mallacca would be any the wiser or worry about it even if they knew. This would come to a tidy sum, for a thousand guests had paid a thousand dollars a couple for the pleasure of the dinner and the subsequent entertainment. Raffles would follow, husbands get lost, wives make hasty liaisons with fishermen decked out in livery. Angelica would arrange special bookings, give cards to those who hadn't heard about her enterprise. Fist fights would occur, hangovers prepared for the following day, a dozen couples would decide on divorces. And the starving children of Africa, the beneficiaries of the gala, would be sent rice, cans of soup, sardines, tuna, wheat, corn-meal, frozen Argentine beef, and other such delicacies to tempt discerning palates.

There were some unusual, not to mention unexpected couplings on the ride to the palace.

The Mercedes carried Arki and Toni; the Rolls, Deborah and Brian Teal. Nick rode with John Mulholland in an Austin Princess. Nazem found himself in his Bentley with his young friend, Gavin Southwell.

Fritz von Kuhl accommodated only one passenger in his Ferrari, Maureen Polley. His aristocratic gallantry had expired and he didn't care if Madeleine had to call a cab or walk. He was determined to ignore her as skillfully as she had ignored him in the past.

Thomas Ambrose-Smith, after a long retching episode in Toni's *bain privé,* had gained control of his fragmented mind and accepted a ride from Carla and Giovanni in their spanking new Jensen F.F. Madeleine and Victoria slid into the back of someone's black Rolls, and in the confusion for transport, Ricardo Ricci and Jacques de Charlus jumped in.

The cortège, horns honking joyfully, proceeding at a speed of five kilometers an hour, joined the end of the line on the Coronet Walk which was choked with traffic despite the movements of an ambitious director of traffic safety who dealt ambiguous signals with the skill of a Las Vegas blackjack dealer.

At the head of the receiving line, Susan and Paul stood shaking hands, embracing friends and enemies alike, and positively affable to each other. The cool control was the first stage of Susan's plan. As Arki leaned forward to kiss her, she whispered in his ear:

"Let's meet in the Orangerie later. I've got to speak to you."

Not wishing to appear conspicuous or even remotely suspicious of Paul, he laughed.

"Of course we're happy," he said for the benefit of anyone who might overhear, and nodded assent to Susan.

Paul managed to exchange pleasantries with Arki. Arki's attitude with Paul was so matter of fact that Paul was reassured and silently congratulated himself for outsmarting him. Who would have believed it? Everyone always wrote Paul off as a lightweight, more concerned with the fit of his jacket than with politics or finance. The know-nothing dandy, dressed to the nines, who couldn't tell one end of a balance sheet from the other, had brought off the coup of the century. Apart from the effect on Paul's ego, it would certainly bring new admiring members of the world's business community into his orbit. The action, which under normal circumstances would make him *persona non grata,* would, because it was leveled against Arki, make him famous, sought-after, for Arki had created waves of hostility among bankers, company presidents and brokerage firms. They'd all pat Paul on the back and say that Arki deserved it, and wasn't it nice to have someone pay him back in kind at long last.

Arki had not yet found a way to counter Paul's dreams of glory. After a frantic conference with his advisers, he had alerted financial sources in New York, Paris, London and Zurich that Mallacca was about to announce bankruptcy and was on the point of nationalizing the property and assets of foreign nationals. But since Mallacca's international debts were minimal, this merely stopped the limited credit that the country had and did little to help Arki personally, for he himself was the principal creditor. For hours Arki had wrestled with the problem but had found no way out, either legal or illegal. Short of taking over the country with Congo mercenaries—and he had seriously considered it—there was no way he could alter the movement of destiny. The other practical solution that he had toyed with was the removal by assassination of Paul. But this would have made him liable to blackmail, or even worse, possible conviction. Even Nazem had not been assassinated. He had been allowed to escape his country when it was in the hands of a military dictatorship,

and no more tyrannical and corrupt monarch had sat on a throne
since the Borgias. So what would world opinion be if a charming, graceful playboy had been removed?

Arki still pondered the problem while greeting old friends and
proudly showing off Toni, whose dress was the most magnificent
among the entire assembly at the gala. To save anything, he'd
have to move quickly, and he had given orders to get the boat
outside the three-mile limit as soon as his guests returned. There
was no reason why Paul could not enjoin the boat as well. It
would be a simple matter for Paul to cut off the lines of communication from Mallacca to the outside world, appoint a censor,
and then announce that a state of emergency had been declared
and that Archimedes Pendelos had been plotting to overthrow
him. What was more, the world would believe Paul, since no
one could imagine him acting on anything unless the palace itself
was burning. The papers would publish Paul's releases, indicating
Arki's Mallaccan holdings, and the political situation of the
tiny country would become the object of sympathy of governments everywhere. No, there was nothing for it, but to run under
cover of darkness.

"I think it's going all right," Toni said. "Paul was so pleasant.
I can't believe he'd try to hurt you."

"When Frank was sitting in Paris with the Russians, didn't
you think that these nice civilized men wouldn't really use atomic
weapons? Wasn't the magnitude of it more than you could
imagine?"

"Yes," she admitted. "One of them—Vronski—was a classics
scholar just like Frank . . ."

"And what was Frank's attitude?" Arki asked.

"That if he turned his back they'd stick a knife in it."

"Frank was a good bargainer and knew his people well. But
you drank cocktails with them, danced at a ball with them, and
they seemed to you urbane and sensible and if I'm not mistaken
you said in an interview that they were really the last of the
gallant gentlemen."

"Oh, Arki, I am naive." And then she asked, "Is it hopeless, darling?"

He frowned and rubbed his mechanical arm. "I'll survive Paul Martell and one day come back and eat him alive."

He led her out to the dance floor. The Flying Caterpillars, a noisy new English group, were blasting out their version of "Hey Jude." Arki, after the Latin American dances became passé, had been instructed in the Twist and Frug, and although he still felt a bit uncomfortable, he moved with reasonable assurance. Toni loved the new dances, and with her eyes partly closed gyrated like a teenager.

"I prefer making love," Arki said when she got close.

"This isn't a bad substitute for the moment."

A gallery of people had formed to watch them as though viewing a golf tournament.

From time to time she picked up snatches of conversation.

"It won't last," said an Italian prince who had pursued her with success in Rome.

"She'll make him pay plenty. Have you seen the ring?" asked the professional starlet with him.

"I'm going to cut in and try to slip it off her finger."

Toni opened her eyes and danced to the center of the floor to avoid him.

"Don't let anyone cut in," she asked Arki.

"The Italian?"

"Uh-huh. Can't stand him."

As they made an effort to move away, Fritz wrapped an arm around Arki's shoulder.

"Can I steal him for a minute?"

"Important?"

"Something you ought to hear about."

Arki bowed his head to Toni like a seventeenth-century cavalier.

"Darling, excuse me for a minute. I won't be long."

Mulholland caught Arki's signal a moment too late, and the Italian began to dance opposite her.

"In Rome, do you remember, Toni?"

"How could I forget your cologne."

"I changed it after you complained." He tried to put his arms around her and she moved away deftly. "We had a pleasant evening."

He'd been merely a one-night stand to her; she'd have to be careful.

"I'm going to get married."

"Everyone's talked of nothing else all day. Still, Toni, you lose interest quickly. And Archimedes is a busy man."

"Not too busy for me," she said curtly.

"Let's wait and see, shall we? In any case, I'm available for any small service you may require."

With the appearance of the orchestra, the music changed to a waltz, and Toni was relieved to have Mulholland cut in.

"God, John, I thought you'd never get here."

"Sorry, my love, I thought you were enjoying yourself."

"John, don't think. When you're called, come. And don't ever let that bastard get near me!"

Arki and Fritz had moved to a corner of the ballroom to avoid eavesdroppers.

"You won't believe this, Arki, but this afternoon I had a visit from Paul's minister for contracts. He put a proposition to me. Apparently they'd like us to build a steel factory here. I was shown pictures of the site they have in mind. The Spanish Village."

"What were you offered?" Arki asked, biting his lower lip.

"Various trading concessions and land for development. I thought it all a practical joke. When I said the cost was likely to be anywhere between two and three hundred million dollars for such a project, I thought I'd discouraged Baguette—that's his name. But he didn't even blink. I made some remark about the fact that Von Kuhl won't accept Eau de Mallacca or Casino chips in payment, and he assured me that they were prepared to put half the sum down and either pay off over ten years or give me concessions. Whichever I preferred."

"Did you believe him?" Arki asked.

"Not at the beginning, but then it occurred to me that since you and Paul are so close, somehow you must be behind the project and of course I was interested. It couldn't possibly be Paul—his expertise is confined to the Frug. So my friend, what do you say? Shall I telephone Berlin and get a team of engineers and cost analysts over?"

"If I were you, Fritz, I'd wait."

"What?" He was incredulous. "You mean to say you aren't involved in this?"

"No, and I don't intend being involved."

"Then what the devil have they in mind? Paul can't even pay his tailor. This is absurd. I can assure you that Baguette is no fool because he had various estimates with him. One from a Swedish cartel and one from Vickers."

Susan, at some distance, made an effort to catch Arki's eye but he shook her off. He was in no mood to listen to gossip or give advice about how to cope with Paul's philandering. But Susan was insistent and slipped through the milling throng of guests to get to him.

She paused a few feet from the two men and said something that Arki could not hear because of the din.

"I think you're being called," Fritz said.

"I'm in no mood for social pleasantries or chitchat. Can you rescue me?"

Before Fritz could reply, Susan came closer and gave him a piercing look.

"Now, Arki, it's important!" she said.

"Is it really important, Susan?" Something in her manner convinced him it was. Susan hurried away, expecting him to follow.

"I'll explain to Toni," Fritz said.

"Oh, well, I'll only be a few moments," Arki said with irritation.

He found Susan standing by a doorway.

"Just follow me quickly, Arki."

"What is this mystery?"

"Just trust me."

"Yes, I know where that will get me."

The passageway was heavy with dust and the walls damp to the touch, and he wondered for an instant if he were being led into a trap. Anything was possible with these people. He felt nervous and disarmed and he reached out through the darkness and touched Susan's shoulders.

"It's all right," she said, pushing open a heavy door.

There was a smell of flowers and sweet-smelling fruit and she turned on the light.

"I thought you wanted to meet later," he said looking around the Orangerie which was little-used and seemed rather sinister. "I haven't told Toni that I've left," he added uneasily.

"We won't be long. And after you've heard what I've said, you won't be sorry."

"Well, what's so important?"

"Your personal fortune in Mallacca. Or perhaps it isn't," she said quickly.

"What do you know about it?"

"I know Paul's plans for relieving you of it."

"So do I. And I'm sure there's a basis of negotiation."

"Not with him. With me."

"I don't understand, Susan. Is this some kind of blackmail? People simply don't go around seizing other people's property. Especially mine! If anyone is responsible for the new prosperity in this place, it's me."

"You don't have to recite your accomplishments to me. We're not in court."

He decided on a different tack. Possibly she had a way out for him, but it seemed unreasonable that she'd undermine Paul.

No, there was something more, so there must be some possibility that everything wasn't watertight.

"Paul is going to nationalíze your property and freeze your assets."

"If you've got any influence with him I'd strongly urge you to tell him to reconsider. Obviously, I'm not going to let him just take what doesn't belong to him without reprisals."

He was a specialist in the veiled threat, the long look, the little ambiguous smile. These little tricks in negotiation often made the other person either show his hand or else back off. Exploiting other people's fears without actually saying anything was an art that Arki had practiced for thirty years with remarkable success. It took as a principle the theory employed in Judo—using the other fellow's weight and size to force him down. Say as little as possible directly but imply. That was the key. Imply that you had alternatives without mentioning them, imply that you weren't really interested, imply that you had the advantage, even if there was none. In a battle of equals, the winner depended on his opponent's mistakes. Arki had never before been under so much pressure and this increased the degree of his calmness and brought out his ruthless skill. It wasn't yet time for a diversionary maneuver. He'd have to wait until she showed her hand.

"By noon tomorrow, Arki, everything you own will belong to Paul under a nationalization plan .which is quite legal and in accordance with the constitution of Mallacca."

"We'll see about that, won't we?"

"You're bluffing. You haven't got a hope and you know it."

"Don't forget that I'm a representative of a foreign power and that I don't entirely own everything that Paul says I do. All of it is in the names of my companies. And these companies have directors who are French, German, English, Dutch, Turkish and so on. And obviously they aren't going to take this like little sheep."

"I am the daughter of a self-made multimillionaire and I've

seen my father use the same kind of tactics. You're completely powerless unless I help you."

"I assume that your services aren't being given in the name of fair play or Christian idealism," he replied with a snigger. But at the same time he had caught something new in Susan's attitude. Yes, she was different.

"We all have a price," she said.

"Murdering Paul is out of the question."

"Of course it is. I want to see him die slowly. I've thought of a variation of the Indian water death. It would be an amusing spectacle to see Paul without money, wouldn't it?"

"He's always without money. People have stopped laughing since they've become creditors. We all wish him a long life and hope for prompt payment."

"Did you know that the Countess of Mallacca has certain powers that are guaranteed by law, and that work quite independently of the Count?"

Now it was becoming interesting and Arki's brown eyes gleamed. Yes, she was planning to draw and quarter Paul.

"I had often wondered how long you would tolerate Angelica."

"You can stop wondering," she said sharply.

"No one enjoyed the spectacle. Paul never deserved anyone like you. He would have been better off, Count or not, with a common streetwalker. We tolerated Paul for your sake."

"Thank you." Ice could not have been colder than her words.

He gave a little bow, wholly fascinated by what was being revealed to him.

"The law that Paul plans to use is an Enabling Act and you're familiar with the extraordinary powers this can give a head of government," Susan said in a businesslike manner that more than impressed him. "There is a special proviso, however, that they've added—he and Baguette—in order to prevent a national revolution. It calls for a token tax to be paid by Mallaccan citizens who are property owners and of course this won't be enforced, since the whole nationalization program is directed against you."

"I assumed that this might be the case. He'd use my property and funds to build a few schools and a hospital to quiet criticism and then keep the rest for himself."

"Arki, let's talk about the future. Under a special dispensation the Countess of Mallacca can give citizenship to anyone she chooses to. This was formerly a ceremonial act, but it's perfectly legal and its intention was to aid people unjustly accused by their own countries."

"Are you certain that it's legal?" he asked, controlling himself with difficulty.

"I've done it three times before. Signed my name on an immigration form."

He had now, he realized, to make her an offer for her part. She wouldn't accept a flat sum.

"I think it's only fair that you accept some assistance from me. You'll have to leave Mallacca undoubtedly and you'll need some funds. Half my share of the Casino proceeds for five years would see you through."

"Ten percent of your entire holdings in Mallacca and passage on the *Archimedes* to France."

He hesitated and she looked sternly at him. "You've got ten seconds to make up your mind. Ninety percent of something is better than a hundred percent of nothing!"

"Agreed!"

"My share comes to fourteen million dollars," she said.

"Who said you were just a pretty face?"

"Probably Paul."

The crowding at the bar was like the rush hour on a subway, and Brian in the mass of flesh found Deborah's hand.

"I don't know where anyone is," she said.

"Don't let that bother you."

She gave him a long honeyed look and squeezed his fingers.

"Why don't we get a bit of air," he suggested.

"That's a brilliant idea, Brian."

"Beach all right?"

"Yes. No one's going to miss us for a while."

By the time the guests had reached the main course everyone had agreed that this was surely the greatest gala in Mallacca's history. Certainly it was one of the most colorful. Fabricio himself had arrived two days before to direct the final decorations in the Grand Ballroom. Of course he had changed everything, to the delight of Susan. The room had been done in a blend of the old and new. Crystal chandeliers and mirrors married well with the subtle bunting and floral designs that were Fabricio's specialty. Wall fountains, of the sort that offer holy water in churches, gurgled champagne. A corps of luscious girls in minuscule attire wove dangerously through the throng carrying appetizers that would have done credit to the great Soulé himself. Their insouciance in the face of pats, strokes, pinches and other hazards was marvelous to behold. Never before had there been such beautiful girls, or for certain members, such lovely boys. Ambrose-Smith smacked his lips in relish as he surveyed the scene.

Nazem had bent every effort to induce Susan to allow him to be in charge of the "entertainment." She had resisted, though with difficulty. For, indeed, something in her wanted his strange and certainly unique hand in the proceedings. She felt the need to shock, to make this a gala everyone would remember out of all the galas. She would certainly remember it; but others must too.

"I have some simply adorable films, my dear," Nazem had said, stroking her with his liquid eyes.

"I'm sure you have, but you know I think this is hardly the time."

He chortled, a tinge of pink coming to his enormous chins. "You must learn to be bold, my dear Susan."

"Perhaps I shall."

And never had the cuisine been so exactly *au point*. Seven soups were offered, including an absolutely superb bird's nest soup created by Hong Fow at Bouillard's in St. Germain and flown in for the gala. Duck, goose (for Fritz of course), woodcock flown from Scotland. Truffles from the hand of Pointe himself. And to cap everything off Demel's in Vienna, the one and only Demel's, had sent an assortment of pastry that would have driven Franz Josef himself into an ecstasy of salivation. As one joyous gourmet observed, not since the Congress of Vienna had there been such a collection of culinary talent employed for the pleasures of the body.

"What a marvelous way to go bankrupt," said Mulholland as he stroked his stomach. "The sauces alone would make a chef's reputation."

Even the musicians were great. Between dances they broke into groups and serenaded individual tables. Charlie Springs had come all the way from Vegas to sing, and when music and song had momentarily satiated the guests, there was Tony Sellers, "Tone the Bone," to regale them with the funniest and dirtiest stories.

As the main course was cleared masked tumblers suddenly flung themselves onto the stage and did a fantastic striptease with cartwheels, backflips, handstands and the like. The climax brought a crescendo of applause as it was revealed that the male tumblers were female, and the women tumblers were actually men. Naked but still masked (a point appreciated by Nazem), they linked arms and chain-danced among the tables.

It was, as a dignitary from some country observed, good clean fun for a good, clean cause.

Marta stood in the wings and observed the party at Arki's table. The lights were low and she could see but not be seen.

She listened to the close of Sir Arthur Kenika's speech about the malnutrition and starvation that African children were subjected to. Sir Arthur in the red ceremonial robes of his nation said that he hoped he would hear no applause when he concluded, since the assembly would be putting their hands in their pockets or filling in the blank checks which were to be found just beside the floral centerpiece. He began quoting some statistics and Marta leaned through the curtain. Those at Arki's table all had their backs to the curtain, and she located Toni and placed a half-opened capsule in her wineglass. She watched the powder dissolve and then left her place and slipped through the long passageway which led to the wings. It was bare and cold, but Marta felt warm with satisfaction. At last everyone would see Antonia Millhouse as she really was. The empty, vain, man-eating bitch.

The orchestra played the music for Marta's entrance, and as she moved gracefully onto the stage like a white rose timelessly captured in a bell jar, she heard a shriek.

No one in the ballroom was certain who had screamed or what had happened. Some of the guests began to laugh, thinking that a practical joke was being played by someone. For, except for the spotlight on Marta, the hall was plunged in darkness. But again there was a scream, this time piercing and terrifying. Chairs were pushed back and then a woman was seen to be running. Voices were raised in protest at this behavior. Yet through it all Marta continued her performance.

Several other people rushed from the ballroom. Arki was appalled. Toni wasn't in the grand salon where they had had drinks before dinner. What could have gone wrong? Mulholland and Nick as well as Gavin burst through the door and found Arki. There was a look of anger on his face.

"Where did she go?" he demanded. He wasn't going to accept this kind of behavior from anyone, not even Toni.

"I don't know. What happened? Did anyone see?"

"It doesn't make sense," said Nick. "She asked me to light her cigarette and then started to scream. I saw her eyes. She looked insane."

"Oh shut up, Nick!" Arki said coldly.

"I'm telling you the truth. Her eyes. I've never seen anyone like that."

"May I suggest that we look for her instead of discussing theories," Mulholland said.

"Someone go into the ladies' room and see if she's there," Arki ordered.

They waited for a few moments, carefully avoiding one another's eyes.

"Maybe it's those diet pills she takes," Gavin suggested.

"Oh for once don't be an ass," Arki snapped.

"I don't have to take that kinda talk from you or anyone, hear," Gavin said, turning beet-red.

"She isn't in the john," Mulholland said.

"By why in God's name would she do such a thing?" Arki asked no one in particular.

There was a guilty silence and then the group filed out the front door where the chauffeurs were chatting.

"Did anyone see Madame Millhouse come out?" Arki said.

"Yes," said a chauffeur, moving into the light. "She ran past me and I saw her turn toward the Coronet."

"I want you to go along the front . . . the Coronet," Arki said.

Running. Running.

Lights out of focus.

Blurs.

Colors changing.

Lamplights green, then red.

Must keep moving.

Tears thick as molasses.

Can't open my eyes.

Sand under my feet.

The sound of water.

Dress getting wet.

Ears hurt.

Lights coming from the sea.

Boats?

Where am I?

Smell of salt.
The inside of my head.
My brain.
I can see it.
It's a mass of wires.
Blood-red.
Crisscrossing.
Soft bloody putty inside.
Walking around.
I'm starting to choke.
God, I'm dying.
I've been poisoned!
I've got to force myself to vomit.
Two fingers down my throat.
Oh, my stomach hurts.
I want my daddy.
My parents didn't touch.
Archimedes said . . .
What did he say?
Give me a lever and I will lift the earth.
Why am I thinking of Archimedes?
What does it mean?
Running again.
Running.
Where to?
Oh, I do like boats so much.
They make me feel safe.
I see a sea wall.
Slime on my feet.
They're bleeding.
Don't feel a thing.
God, I'm dead.

"There's someone there," Deborah said. "God, Brian we've been seen!"

Brian paid no attention and continued to fondle her breasts.

"You've got to stop," she insisted.

"I can't. I'm almost there. Another minute."

"It's a woman in an evening dress." She gasped in horror when she recognized Toni, not more than twenty yards from them.

"It's Toni."

"She wants everything you have."

"You're right. Look, she's walking away. Something must be wrong."

"Let her sort it out, love."

"Oooh. Ooooooh. Don't stop. Not now. Oooo, I need this."

"I love your box. It's so tight."

"I'm coming," Deborah said and held him so tightly that he winced.

"Hey, baby, leave some for next time."

The Mercedes 600 stopped at the side of the Carlton. The chauffeur was ordered to proceed to the *Archimedes* with Gavin and wait. If Toni was there they'd come back for the others.

"Nick, come with me," Arki said. "John, you take that side of the street by the beach."

"If we find her we'll meet you at the hotel," Mulholland said.

"I don't think she'd go back to the boat on foot," said Nick.

"Nick, stop thinking! Get on the phone and call the chief of police. Tell him that I want him personally with a search party to meet me in front of the Carlton in exactly ten minutes."

"That's not giving him very much time."

"Just do as you're told," Arki said with exasperation. "I pay his salary."

The two men entered the lobby of the Carlton and went to the concierge's desk, but were told that Toni had not come in. She would have been noticed, since things were very quiet and everyone was at the gala. In the American Bar they spoke to the barman who was serving two women. The gala crowd wouldn't arrive till after two, they were informed by the barman, and no, these were the only two people in the bar.

The concierge rushed into the bar to tell Arki that he was wanted on the telephone. He picked up the bar phone and prayed that it would be Toni.

"She's not on the boat," Gavin said at the other end. "The duty officer would have seen her if she'd come back."

"Well, you just stay there," Arki said. "She might return."

"Anyone see her at the hotel?"

"No." He hung up, looked at Nick who shrugged his shoulders regretfully.

"It was so fast . . . the way she ran out. We came after her a minute later. I think we've made a mistake. She couldn't have got this far. Let's go back to the palace."

"I'll go. You wait for the police and tell them I said that they should search the beach."

The concierge put Arki into a waiting taxi and he returned to the palace grounds. People were milling around the gardens and entrance. Arki spotted Fritz and Giovanni, and he rushed up to them.

"Have you seen Toni?"

"No," said Fritz. "What happened? People are in a state of shock about her screaming."

"Is she all right?" asked a concerned Giovanni.

"I don't know. She became ill as Marta started to dance."

"The gossips are saying that she's a drug addict," Fritz said.

"Let's look around the grounds," Giovanni said.

"Perhaps she's gone to the Casino," Fritz suggested. "It's only on the next street."

"I never thought of that," Arki said.

"Will you go ahead and if you find her, call the boat and get my doctor there at once?"

"Yes, of course," said Fritz.

Marta came toward him and Arki was struck by her cool, detached manner. Jacques held her arm and she looked more desirable than ever in a low-cut, black sequined gown.

"I know you never cared very much for the ballet, but I thought Toni was all for art," she said.

"She was suddenly taken ill," Arki explained.

"You'd better look after her. She isn't quite as hardy as the other flowers," Marta said, turning abruptly away to accept the congratulations of the various ballet directors who were falling over themselves to get near her.

Arki walked to the rear of the palace. A few couples had paired off and slunk into the bushes. Toni was not there.

Arki's appearance at the Casino caused a flurry of excitement. The Casino manager tried to usher him into his private office. Already the crowd was there and the wheels were busy as well as the chemin de fer tables. Americans lined the crap table.

"I'm looking for Madame Millhouse," Arki said.

"Madame Millhouse?" the manager asked in return. "No, not since yesterday when you brought her in. Did you want to see the books?" the manager asked.

"No, I don't, you idiot," Arki barked.

"I'm sorry, Monsieur Pendelos, I thought you did."

"Look, if she turns up, phone me at the boat and I'll return."

Arki bowed his head, worried and exhausted. For a moment he seemed almost human to the manager.

The sound of water.
A continual movement.
Far off.
Now closer.
Imprisoned in this armor.
I can't breathe.
If I can only move my hands.
Snaps are moving.
Oh, thank God, I can breathe.
What was I wearing?

It weighed a ton.

Shining brightly like gold in the sunlight.

I'm lying on the sand.

Are they going to bury me alive?

Please don't.

Can't you hear me?

A party was in full swing when Arki and Nick returned to the boat. A crowd of people, most of whom he didn't know, had commandeered the main deck and were wildly gyrating to the music of the Flying Caterpillars who had performed earlier at the gala. Gavin caught sight of him and hurtled through the dancers.

"Where's Toni?"

"The police haven't found her yet," Nick said.

"The police can't even find the jail here," Arki said. "I'll organize the crew." He signaled the captain and briefly explained the situation; the captain acted quickly, forming a party of twenty-five seamen to begin a search.

Armed with flashlights and first-aid kits they divided up the area into ten sections and headed down the Coronet Walk and the beaches. Arki retired to his cabin to think. Why was he here, he asked himself. He should be out looking for Toni. And yet he knew that everything was being done that could be done. He stood in the cabin feeling frustrated and enraged at his own impotence in the face of this calamity. Damn! Whom could he call? What could he do! In a fury, he went into his office, the only quiet place aboard, for there were people swarming through the salon and he didn't have the energy to protest. He must think; he must keep cool.

He jumped back in alarm when he saw someone sitting in his chair. He turned on the light and discovered Susan with her eyes closed, the picture of serenity.

"Where've you been? I've been waiting an hour," she said.

"How'd you get here so quickly?"

"I just left in my car. Now that I have only myself to worry about, I do as I please."

"Did you see Toni?" he asked hopelessly.

"No, should I have?"

"Weren't you there during the entertainment?"

"I never bothered to return after our chat. I had your papers to prepare." She opened a folder and presented him with the two documents. One was an official immigration form which she handed him: "Just sign, citizen of Mallacca. The other one is our letter of agreement."

"I could sign and refuse to honor it," he said. "But I won't."

"I prefer to trust you rather than Paul," Susan said.

The noise from the party spilled into the room, and Arki realized that he had left the door open. He was too dispirited and exhausted to move, and he sank into the sofa opposite Susan. He'd saved his fortune and lost Toni and he didn't know quite what to do.

"Arki, what's happened! Where's Toni?" Susan asked, realizing at last that something was the matter.

"God knows where she is. As Marta began to dance, Toni screamed and ran from the ballroom and we can't find her."

Susan sat perfectly still for several moments considering the statement, then she rose and touched Arki's shoulder.

"Maybe she's being punished for stealing what doesn't belong to her."

"Oh—for God's sake. The last thing I need, Susan, is that come-to-Jesus stuff!"

"I'm not being sentimental," Susan said. "I mean it. She's maybe getting hers—as the saying goes."

"Did Marta do something to her? Tell me, Susan, for God's sake!"

"How would I know? I wouldn't put it past her. And I wouldn't blame her."

He stood before her, clenching his one good fist and the veins stood out on his face and neck. "If she has, if she's done this, I'll get that goddamn bitch, so help me!"

"Marta may have done nothing. And if she did, what can you do about it?"

His look answered her.

Susan started out of the cabin and then she stopped. "I hope Toni has learned something from all this, Arki. I know I have."

Walking along the beach I feel free.
I can see lights and people dancing.
Is this hell?
Have I died?
Voices carrying in the wind.
I hear my name.
Someone's calling me.

"We've found her," a man's voice rang out in the darkness. "She's on the beach."

Actually, she was only a hundred yards from the boat, and Arki, prowling the bridge like a cat in a storm, raced down the ladder, then with half a dozen seamen, rushed across the beach.

A flashlight was shining on a woman who was naked, and Arki pulled off his jacket and wrapped it about her. He gathered Toni in his arms. Her skin was cold and she had a numbed, dazed look on her face. Then slowly, and quite without life, she began to cry. Like a smashed doll.

"I want everyone off my boat," Arki ordered the captain. "The party's over. Only my sailing guests can stay. We're weighing anchor."

The doctor confirmed the fact that Toni had been drugged. He was not sure what the drug was; they'd have to do tests, but he thought it might be a derivative of lysergic acid.

The next morning when Toni awakened she had no recollection of the previous night. She was concerned about her dress and when a steward told her that it had been recovered by a search party on the beach, she smiled faintly.

Arki stayed glued to her side. For hours she did not recognize him and he was beside himself. But at last, as he fed her supper on the day following the gala, she saw him. Her eyes suddenly cleared and she smiled.

"Arki . . ."

"Toni, darling."

And then her eyes clouded. "I don't remember . . ."

"It's all right, darling. I am taking care of you."

She reached up and touched the side of his face. "Arki, I love you. I don't know what happened."

His face darkened. "I'll get that bitch Marta if it's the last thing I do."

But she was shaking her head slowly from side to side, as she would have done to a child. "No—no, Arki. It doesn't matter. I-I just want to be with you." Her lips were against his ear. "Get in bed with me."

It all seemed back to normal. More or less. Sunworshippers on deck were enjoying the pool and the drinks of their gracious host. Arki's sailing guests were fairly numerous. Giovanni Mosca and Carla were happy to accept the invitation for a second honeymoon. And Fritz and Maureen were having a pre-honeymoon trial. As usual, John Mulholland tended bar with perfection and made terrific banana daquiris for everyone.

Susan Belmont, still Countess of Mallacca, had discovered that Jacques de Charlus, apart from his skill at designing, was providing more than adequate service for her personal requirements. And for the first time in years she was really devoting herself to the twins. They were with her every moment of the time that she wasn't alone with Jacques. "It's like getting to know them for the first time," she told Arki.

"You are a new woman, Susan," Arki said.

A few people were not at all pleased by the new groupings.

Nick for one became hysterical when he realized that Deborah was serious about an acting career, so serious indeed that she insisted Brian Teal join them on the boat for the rest of the cruise. Ricardo and Madeleine had joined forces in a rather unemotional affair, until something better appeared. And Nazem— Nazem had invited some dainty morsels from Angelica's establishment: two little French things who found his company not only entertaining but instructive. He was sorry to have lost Susan, he told her so at inordinate length, but he was also pleased at his privileged position aboard so that he could witness her new affair with Jacques, as well as the other groupings and couplings.

Meanwhile back on Mallacca, Paul Martell had learned of Arki's recently acquired citizenship at his own press conference. Since it was all quite legal, he had to swallow his tongue and reverse his strategy. He discussed with Angelica the prospect of turning Mallacca into another Capri or Fire Island. She thought the idea a stroke of genius (again!) and assured him that it would present no difficulties to her. That kind of person never caused trouble.

Yes, they were homeward bound. All of them. No one was disillusioned, for illusions didn't exist in their circles. Nor were they disenchanted, since enchantment, like measles, is a disease of childhood. They weren't bruised or battered either—money protected them from that.

Foreskins (for those who had them) were red and gently laid to rest, swathed in cold cream. Nobody got pregnant. Pills, rings, and Dutch bonnets protected the ladies against unwanted issue. Looking back, it had been a happy week, a bit more unusual than previous galas. New experience had been gained, a few fantasies realized, made tangible, and now the search would begin anew in the autumn with the rounds of party-going and party-giving. There might be some new faces, which they'd all welcome. But they'd meet again.

In Bermuda, or Palm Beach, or Acapulco, or London, before going to the snow in magic places—St. Moritz, Innsbruck,

Gstaadt. Tommy suggested the French Alps as a joke. He had a friend there who was a ski instructor. But he failed to reckon with Victoria who had made plans for his attendance at the Commonwealth Games.

Toni, everyone could see, was different. Nobody could quite put a finger on it, but there was something relaxed, more quiet about her. Was she just enjoying her new happiness? Or was she thinking of the opportunity to repay Marta in kind?

Toni stretched on her chaise longue and Arki touched her forehead with a cold towel. Even perspiration mustn't be tolerated.

"Arki."

"Yes, my love."

She smiled at the sea. "Can we live forever?"

"I'll see what I can do about it," he said. It was a thought that had never before occurred to him.

THIS BOOK WAS SET IN

CALEDONIA AND OUTLINE GOTHIC TYPES

AND BOUND BY

AMERICAN BOOK-STRATFORD PRESS, INC.

IT WAS PRINTED BY

MURRAY PRINTING COMPANY.

THE DESIGN IS BY

LARRY KAMP AND JULIAN HAMER